Divine Intervention When God Steps In

Liv N. Love

Published by Liv N. Love, 2025.

This is a work of fiction. Similarities to real people, places, or events are entirely coincidental.

DIVINE INTERVENTION WHEN GOD STEPS IN

First edition. March 9, 2025.

Copyright © 2025 Liv N. Love.

ISBN: 979-8230752318

Written by Liv N. Love.

All honor, praise and glory to God. I could not have done any of this without His guidance, and inspiration.

Prologue

" Momma, momma, guess what happened at school today! I made a new friend!" Faith couldn't wait to tell her mother of this exciting new development.

Julie, Faith's mother, gave her a very big hug. " That's wonderful sweetheart! Let's get our hot cocoa, and then you can tell me all about it."

Faith was so excited to tell her mom all about her new friend. She was almost bouncing out of her seat, waiting for her mom to get settled.

Julie had hardly gotten settled before Faith launched into her story on how they became friends. Julie sat and listened to the entire story, smiling at this amazing gift she has been blessed with, and her heart was full of so much love. She silently thanked God again for the miracle of Faith.

"Can you believe that momma?" Faith asked after she had finished with her exciting story.

" Sounds like divine timing that you were right there to meet, and help your new friend."

" What's divine timing momma?" Faith had never heard this phrase before, and she didn't know what it meant.

" It's just something I was told before that stuck with me. It's when God puts you in the right place at the right time. It's meant to be as part of our journey in life." Julie smiled with such love in her eyes, yet the memory of the first time she was told about this was fresh in her mind.

" I like that momma. Can I say it too?"

" If you truly understand what it means, and you feel God's hands in the timing, then you most definitely can." Julie loved seeing this curious and loving side of her little miracle girl.

Faith then looked for things that she could use the wonderful phrase, divine timing, throughout each day.

Somehow through the years Faith had forgotten about the phrase given to her by her mother. Faith let a lot of the wonderful things her mother shared with her, fade from her thoughts. It had become too painful after the passing of her mother.

Faith was in her late teens when her mom first got sick, and by Christmas she was gone. Just before Faith turned eighteen years old.

The cancer diagnosis threw their entire lives upside down. All the plans they had made for graduation and college just didn't seem that important any longer. Faith went to school yet, as her mother refused to let her illness steal anymore, of Faith's childhood, than it was going to in the end.

Faith would come straight home from school, and take care of her mom up until she went to bed each night. The weekends were always spent with her mom as well. Most of the time they'd just visit about her day, other times Faith would read some of her mom's favorite books to her. They both knew Julie's time was coming to an end, and they tried to spend their time together with love and joy, as hard as it was. Julie refused to let Faith grieve for her before she was even gone.

It was the last day of school before Christmas break, and Faith was so happy that she'd just get to spend each day with her mom. They had a hospice nurse that sat with her mom while she was at school. Faith appreciated having her there to care for her mother, but she was hoping durning the break that it would be just the two of them.

She came inside the front door, and just knew something horrible was about to happen. The house was always quiet, but today it was deathly quiet.

The hospice nurse was sitting in the living room when Faith came in, and the look on her face told Faith that her mom was gone, yet her heart refused to believe it. She ran to her mom's room expecting to see her still there. Instead she saw an empty room. They had already removed all her mother's medical equipment and the hospital bed. Faith could herself angry!

How dare they just remove it all, like her mom hadn't just been there in the morning when she left for school? How dare they take her mom away without even letting her see her one more time?

The hospice nurse, Ann, explained that her mom passed as peacefully as possible. Ann said her mom knew she wasn't going to make it through the day, and requested that everything be taken care of before Faith got home, as Julie thought it would make it even harder on Faith to see it all be taken away. Before Ann left she made sure Faith had someone on the way to be with her, and she relied the last thing her mother said, as she promised Julie she'd tell Faith.

Even Ann was crying as she shared Julie's message to Faith. " She will be watching over you from heaven, and she knows that you'll be ok, because she raised you to be strong, smart, and independent. She wanted you to know that out of everything in her life, you are her greatest pride and joy. She loves you always, and never doubt that. She asked that you keep with your plans for college, and that you live a happy and love filled life."

It was the worst Christmas of Faith's life. Instead of grieving the loss of her mom, she just got angry, and hated all things Christmas. It didn't seem fair to have everyone she knew, celebrating with family, while she was having to bury her mother. The sorrow was too much for her to face, and she decided that she would work hard to make sure she never felt like that again.

Some pains just seemed too hard to ever deal with; for Faith the loss of her mother was one of those pains. To block out that pain, Faith also ended up blocking all the cherished times they had. She lost a big part of herself by blocking everything related to her mother, but she managed to carry on with day to day. The sadness of not having her mother, invaded her very heart, leaving her with a deep and lasting sorrow. That she carried for many years.

Chapter One

Ten Years Later:

" Ugh, it's already starting. I hate this time of the year!" Faith mumbled to herself as she walked pass a Christmas display. " It's not even December yet!"

She was annoyed, and shaking her head as she went around the corner. She wasn't paying much attention, and her cart slammed right into an elderly man.

The man fell, hitting his head as he landed on the floor, so an ambulance was called.

Faith felt horrible, and just knew she had to follow the ambulance to the hospital. She, thankfully, had overheard the gentleman's name when the EMTs were working on him, so she knew who to ask for when she walked to the front desk.

" Hello, I'm here to see Mathew Gospel. He was brought here by an ambulance." Faith asked the lady manning the front desk.

" Are you family?" The receptionist asked.

Faith knew it was her job, and also knew that she would not get to see him or get any information if she said no. She instantly decided it was much too important to risk, so she said that she was his family. Thankfully the receptionist didn't question her further.

She directed Faith to the room the perfect stranger was put in, after the doctors had admitted him. She stepped into the room quietly, and unsure. She didn't really know what she was going to say beyond how sorry she was.

" Well, hello, young lady. You look like you need something. Can I help you?" Mr. Gospel asked with warmth and compassion.

" Can you please forgive me?" Faith had tears in her eyes.

" I'm sure I can, but may I ask for what I'm forgiving you?"

" I wasn't paying attention at the store, and I ran into you with my cart, as I went around the corner. I was moving way too fast, and was being careless. I am so very sorry." Faith said as a few tears slid silently down her cheeks.

Mathew could see this young woman had so much sorrow within her heart, and knew he had to do what he could to help her. He knew this accident was part of a much bigger picture now. He would honor this, and make a difference if he could. No one should be carrying this much sorrow within their heart.

" Why don't you come on over, and have a seat? It seems we have some talking to do. If you'll do me the honor of your company."

Faith knew she owed him so much more, and would make sure to do whatever she could to make things right. She could not believe what her carelessness and annoyance had caused. Faith slowly walked to the side of the bed, and took a seat. She didn't realize that she was holding her breath until Mathew said that she was.

" Accidents happen, please relax and take a breath. There's nothing to forgive. I'll be just fine. It's just a little concussion. They're just wanting to keep me here, because I'm an old man." He reached out his hand to her.

Faith gently took his hand, and took a deep breath. Then for reasons unknown to her she started crying.

Mathew just continued to hold her hand in his, and silently prayed for the guidance to help her.

" I'm sorry for crying. I don't know where that came from. I guess I was just so afraid that I badly hurt you." Faith said as she got a grip on her emotions.

" No need to apologize my young friend. Sometimes we just need to let our feelings out, and that's just fine. My dear wife would have said it's just fine to cry, but it's also healthy to allow yourself to feel them. How about we start with your name young lady." Mathew gave her hand a gentle squeeze before letting go.

" Oh my, yes, where have my manners gone? My name is Faith. It's nice to meet you, although I wish it wasn't because of my thoughtless cart driving."

" Better a cart, than a car." Mathew said with a small chuckle. He was hoping his small attempt at humor would help her relax and feel better.

Faith couldn't help but to smile. " I can't argue with that logic."

" That's more like it. Now how about a nice chat. I'd appreciate the company." Mathew said glad that she was more relaxed and able to smile.

" Of course, I'd be happy to keep you company. Is there anyone else I can call for you?" Faith didn't know if any of his family or friends had been called.

" I appreciate the offer, but there is no one to call. My dear wife passed away a few months ago, and we were never blessed with any children. I won't be keeping you from anything or anyone, will I?"

" Oh no. I have no plans. I can stay and visit for as long as you'd like. It's the very least I can do, and I would enjoy a nice conversation myself. I was not in the best mood, which is why I wasn't paying attention, and crashed into you." Faith realized she was over sharing.

" I hope you don't mind me prying, but what was weighing on your mind, and ruining your mood?"

" It's kind of silly really, but it's not even December, and Christmas items are everywhere." Fatih said feeling ashamed to have let that cause her to hurt another person.

" You don't like Christmas?" Mathew felt like this was a deeper issue and was willing to listen to get to the real problem, if she would share it.

" Not my favorite season, yet I cannot say I hate Christmas. It just makes me feel more annoyed than anything, and it seems to come earlier and earlier every year." She answered honestly, yet not really saying why.

Mathew knew he had to handle this with "kid gloves," and a ton of love. He didn't want to make her feel uncomfortable.

" My wife just loved everything Christmas, especially the lights. She always said that the lights seemed the most relevant decoration since Christmas is to celebrate the birth of Jesus, so putting more light into the world was a true symbol of Jesus' birth. That's what God did too, by giving us Jesus."

" That's truly beautiful. Hard to not like Christmas lights when said like that." Faith responded, and actually meant it.

Mathew could she he found his opening. Sharing more about his life might help this young lady find her love, and joy again. " Would you like to hear more stories about my lovey? I'd love to share some stories of our life together with you.

Seems like I haven't been able to talk about her and our life in so long."

" I'd be honored." Faith wasn't sure why this seemed so important to Mr. Gospel, but she could tell it was. She couldn't deny him that.

For the next few hours Mathew shared many stories of times with his wife. They both smiled and laughed here and there. They were both enjoying themselves.

When Mathew was getting tired, Faith said she should let him rest, yet she'd be back the next day. She also wrote down her phone number for him, so he could call if he needed anything.

Mathew said how much he looked forward to seeing Faith again the next day.

Chapter Two

The next morning Mathew wasn't sure if Faith would be coming back. Yesterday, he felt certain she would, but he wondered if evil would try to step in and dissuade her from coming back. Mathew did the only thing he knew to do; he prayed.

A couple hours later, he was relieved to see Faith at his door.

" Good morning, Faith! I'm so happy to see you this beautiful morning. I was starting to wonder if I'd get to see you again. It sure does this old man good to have your company."

" Good morning! With such a wonderful greeting like that, you'll have a hard time getting rid of me." Faith said with a smile and wink.

" Why on earth would I want to be rid of you? I haven't had any real visiting since my lovey passed away. You might want to get rid of me, after too many stories."

" Never!" Faith exclaimed, with mocked shock.

That made them both smile. Faith couldn't remember the last time she really smiled like that, or the last time she honestly looked forward to getting together with someone just to visit.

" You, young lady, do an old man's heart wonders." Mathew said truly feeling that way. He had been lonely, but he hadn't realized how much until Faith arrived this morning.

Mathew knew he had a wonderful life, and so much to be grateful; he never complained as he had more than most in his lifetime. Maybe this young lady would be a small way to give back for all he had been blessed. Giving back something into the world since he had been given so much.

" You know Mr. Gospel, I think you're doing more for me with these visits. I don't know why or fully understand this myself, but on my way here, I found myself looking forward to our visit. It's been a while since I looked forward to much of anything. I thank you for that. I hadn't even known that I was missing that in my life." Faith shared just to let him know how much be able to just sit and talk with him, meant to her already.

" It seems our accident was a true blessing, as if we were meant to meet; to help each other, in ways we didn't even know we needed."

Suddenly Faith remembered a phrase and whispered it. " Divine Timing." She had tears in her eyes.

Mathew reached out his hand. He didn't hear what Faith had said, but he could see the pain suddenly in her eyes. " I'm here Faith. You're not alone. What can I do to help ease that pain within your eyes and heart?" Mathew asked almost as a plea.

Faith just gave him a small smile, and held his hand. Then simply said. " Tell me more stories about your life and your lovely wife." She wasn't fully ready to talk about her mother and the pain she still carried due to her passing, but she loved hearing his stories.

" I'd be honored, but will you please do me one thing first?" Mathew replied.

Faith nodded, knowing somehow she could completely trust this wonderful man. It wasn't anything he said or did, yet she could feel it in her gut, and heart that he was someone she could trust.

"When you're able and ready to tell me about it, you'll do so. I feel like that's why you and I were brought together; to help each other. You don't have to carry that pain alone, and maybe I can help carry some of the burden."

" I promise, but how am I helping you? You're in this hospital bed because of me." Faith couldn't imagine how she could be helping him.

" I was a lonely man, and was missing my wife something awful; having you here, being able to share stories about her, and our life together has been healing, and I"m grateful to you for that."

Faith kind of chuckled. " Well then, I'm glad I crashed into you."

Mathew couldn't help but to chuckle as well. He realized that was an odd thing to be grateful, yet it didn't change that fact that he was.

" Can we start with how you met your wife? Then go forward from there? Unless you want to start with your life before you met her. I'd love to hear the entire story, however you want to tell it."

" Oh dear, how much time do you have?" Mathew asked not thinking she'd be free to sit and listen to him for very long.

" I have all day! I work from home, doing medical billing, so I can stay until the end of visiting hours everyday." Faith meant that, and was actually hoping for more time with Mathew. She didn't understand it, but she just knew it was what she wanted.

Now it was Mathew who had tears forming in his eyes. He gave her hand another gentle squeeze, and took a minute to listen for any guidance God wanted to give him.

" I guess I'll start with how I met my dear wife, and go from there." Mathew had a smile of remembrance that shined through his eyes.

" I'd like that. I'd love to get to know your wife more. Sounds like she was a truly amazing person." Faith again just somehow knew that. She wondered if this was ever going to make sense to her, although she knew it didn't matter if it did or didn't.

" That she was. I knew it the moment I first laid my eyes on her. " Mathew smiled more just remembering that first time he saw his wife. After taking a moment to just cherish that memory, he gathered his thoughts to share them with Faith. He wanted to tell their story with all the honor it deserved.

" I knew that she'd be the love of my life that first moment I saw her. In fact I started calling her lovey on our first date. She laughed at first and said why on earth are you calling me lovey? I just told her plain and simple, that she'd be the greatest love of my life, and just calling her love, didn't seem like enough to express that. Oh, she smiled so brightly then, and I called her lovey everyday of our lives together. And she'd smile that same smile every time I did."

" There was this one time, I accidentally called her Lovey in front of a group of people at one of her friend's summer gathering. I hadn't even realized I said it in front of everyone, and when they all just looked at me with that odd look, of shock and amusement, I was a little embarrassed. Lovey though gave me that smile, and I was no longer embarrassed. She loved that I was so in love with her that I called her my special nickname in front of everyone. She told me to call her Lovey in front of everyone any time I want, and she'd beam with pride for having such a loving and wonderful man each time. I was never again ashamed or embarrassed to call her Lovey in public." Mathew's eyes were still so full of love, as he share the story.

Faith loved seeing the light in Mathew's eyes as he started his story of meeting his wife. It made her smile as well.

They sat there together while Mathew shared more stories that went from his life with his wife, to some of his childhood. He shared traditions he learned as a child, and that him and his wife continued throughout their lifetime together. Even though the stories went back and forth Mathew tied them in together, so it made sense going back and forth.

Mathew explained they wanted to have children, but God never blessed them with any. Back in those days medicine wasn't advanced enough to know why, but they remembered that they were blessed more than some, with having each other. As some people didn't have the love and strong relationship they did. He said they tried to be there for others as much as they could. Not having a big family to support, they sometimes were able to help others. They always figured that was, what they were meant to do.

Then he told stories about some of the people they were guided to help, but how at the end of the day it was his wife and himself that got the most out of it. He said that sharing love with others made them feel like they were doing God's work, and that feeling is as close as one can get to understanding the love God feels for His children.

"The gifts meant for others always ended up being a gift back to us. You never know how the love you put out into the world will come back to you, but it always does." Mathew said with deep heartfelt emotions, that Faith could almost feel.

They talked all the way up to lunch. Faith decided that she'd run out, have lunch and do a little work, then come back after Mathew had a little time to rest. She didn't want to wear him out, knowing he needed time to rest as well.

Faith got back to her apartment, and found that she couldn't focus on her work. Her mind kept drifting back to the phrase her mom had thought her, and that day she first learned it, so many years ago. She remembered her mom sitting across the table from her, silently listening to her story over hot cocoa. She remembered her mother's smile for the first time in years.

It was the first time she allowed any memories of her mother, in more years than she could remember. Faith was ashamed and sad.

Was she a bad person for trying to forget her mother? Yet, was she able to handle letting herself remember it all again, including her mother's passing? Questions she didn't know the answers to, and right now she didn't have the time to figure out the answers. She needed to get back to Mr. Gospel.

Faith did not want to make him wait, or think she wasn't coming back to continue their visit, and his stories. Mathew was a natural story teller. They way he described things, and weaved back and forth to tie it all together, was nothing short of amazing. She was really enjoying his stories. Yet honestly, she was so surprised by just how much this time was meaning to her. Guess that's what Mathew meant about being given a gift of love, and having it coming back to you.

When she first said she'd enjoy hearing stories about his wife, she felt like it was what he needed. Yet it's meant so much to her, in ways she never could have imagined.

That's why love is called the greatest gift. She finally understood it. It was the first time she truly believed that it was the greatest gift, and knew why.

It was the one thing anyone could give at any point or time, and it was what everyone needs. It costs nothing to give, yet it is priceless.

Faith shook her head, just stunned. It took her until she was almost 28 years old to know, and understand that. She felt a little unintelligent for a bit, but then she accepted the truth: She denied love and the truth of it since her mother passed away. She let anger take over, and never found her way back. Until now; Mathew was starting to open up her heart, and she didn't even want to fight it. She figured it wouldn't matter that much, because he's only passing through her life.

Suddenly it felt like she just found her mother again, and then lost her all over again. It hit her hard. Why she didn't know, as her mother had been gone for almost ten years now. She didn't think it would still hurt this much. She pulled herself together and headed back to the hospital and Mr. Gospel. Once again refusing to allow her grief to take hold of her.

When she got back to Mr. Gospel's room, she made sure to put on a happy face, which wasn't hard to do, considering she was actually very happy to be back to their visit.

His stories were wonderful to listen to, and she especially enjoyed the love that was still shining in his eyes when he was talking about his wife.

Mathew wasn't worried she wouldn't come back this time. He knew she would, and when she walked in the door, he got a big smile on his face too. He again thanked God for sending Faith to him. He just hoped he was helping her as much as she was helping him.

Mathew realized when she sat down that she had been crying. Yet she didn't look as sad as she was yesterday. That's when he knew he was helping her. Sadly, the way back to love and healing would be a hard one, and tears will fall. He thought of his wife again, and how she said, " Being willing to show and allow tears is a sign of true strength, and trust." He knew Faith would be good in time. By allowing herself to finally feel and deal with those things, she will find her way back to the light.

" Did you have a good lunch?" Faith asked when she sat down.

" I did, even got in a little nap, so we can have another wonderful afternoon. How about you young lady?"

" Oh, yes. I didn't get much work done, but that's fine. I'm ahead of schedule. I can get more done later tonight and in the morning, before I come here to see you." Faith wanted him to know that she would be back again the next day already.

" Do you have any story or things you want to share this time? I don't want to occupy the entire time with my stories, if you want to share any." Mathew asked, hoping she was ready to open up some.

" Oh, I'm completely enjoying hearing your stories. I'm not there yet, but I promised, and I'll let you know when I am ready. Thank you, but please continue." Faith gave him a reassuring smile, and a gentle squeeze of her hand.

They always greeted each other, now with a joining of their hands. Faith thought it was odd that it felt natural with Mr. Gospel. It had never felt natural to even hold hands with the few guys she had dated over the years. For that reason, and many others, Faith had never had a real serious relationship.

" It's my honor, and pleasure." Mathew replied. He didn't want to pressure her. Then he took a moment to gather his thoughts before he started, so he would start from where he had left off at before lunch.

They laughed together at some of the funny parts, and somehow they both seemed to be moved at the same parts of Mathew's stories too. Mathew thought that meant something important, and profound. He just wasn't sure what it all meant yet, but he knew God would let him know when he needed to, if he ever needed to know.

Mathew suddenly was overcome with such a feeling of warmth and love. It was the feeling he knew everyday of his life with his wife. It was at that moment when he knew she had a hand in this. What Mathew didn't know was if it was meant to help him or was there something more to it than just that. His wife always said, " God will put us where we're meant to be at, at the correct times." She called those times Divine Intervention.

" Are you all right Mr. Gospel? Do you need me to get someone?" Faith asked after a few moments after Mathew had gone silent, and was staring off into space, like he wasn't even in the same room as her.

" Oh, I am sorry young lady. I'm just fine, actually I'm better than fine. Just felt the presence of Lovey, in a way." Mathew looked over at her with such love in his eyes.

Faith wondered how someone could have that much love for another person after that long, and even after they passed away. How was he not overcome with anger or grief? Was it because they lived a long life together before she passed?

" I didn't know if I'd ever feel like this again, until I met her in heaven, that is. It's such a wonderful gift, and blessing to be cherished." Mathew continued to say.

The nurse came in just then, and announced visiting hours were over, and it would be best to let Mr. Gospel rest. They hoped he'd be going home the next day, and rest was what was needed most to allow that to happen.

Faith promised to be back there, first thing in the morning, and would be grateful if he would allow her to bring him back to his home when he was released. She wanted to make sure he knew she was going to be there for him after he was released as well.

Mathew was happy to agree to her taking him home. He wasn't in a rush to lose the company. Nor did he think they'd done what was all meant to do to help her either.

Mathew spent the rest of the evening asking God for guidance, and just sitting in silence to hear any answers God was giving him. He knew God was always answering, it's just some times we aren't listening with our hearts and souls to hear those answers.

Chapter Three

Faith made sure to get up early to get a few things done, before heading back to the hospital. That way she could just focus on being there with Mr. Gospel. She got there just before 9am.

" Good morning, Mr. Gospel. How are you feeling this morning?" Faith gave him a big smile. She was surprisingly very happy to be there with him again today. Could it be I'm growing attached to him? She wondered.

" Well, good morning, young lady! With a beautiful greeting, and smile like that how could I be anything but wonderful?" Mathew said with a smile of his own.

" You better watch out Mr. Gospel, if you keep talking to me like that, my ego will be so big that my head won't be able to fit back through the door." Faith said with a good amount of humor.

When was the last time I was humorous about anything? Faith wondered. She wasn't sure what was changing, but spending time with Mr. Gospel was making her feel lighter, and more joyful. She still couldn't understand how that was making such a difference, but it was undeniable, that is was.

Mathew laughed at her ego joke. " You're funny. However I think we have enough room to build up your ego some, and still get you through the door. It is oversized after all for wheel chair access."

Faith had to laugh with him at his joke too.

" Young lady, thank you for that. Been too many days since I started the day with laughter."

" No, thank you! I cannot remember the last time I made a joke or started the day with excitement for that matter. I don't know how or why, but sharing my day with you here, listening to your stories has given me that."

" I happy to hear it's given you those things. I'm sorry you weren't having those feelings before our time together. You're far too young to be so worn down in life." Mathew said. He wanted to ask her more questions to find out why, but still didn't want to push. He hoped someday soon she'd open up on her own. Then hopefully he could help ease the pain from her eyes, and heart completely. At the very least she wouldn't be carrying this burden on her own.

Mathew may have just met her, but he knew a good person when he met one, and she most certainly was one. She deserved to have more love and joy in her life.

Faith didn't know what to say in response, so she just gave him a smile, and sat down.

" Well, am I busting you out of this joint today?" Faith asked.

" I haven't heard just yet, but I do hope so. My house isn't the home it was with Lovey gone, but it's still home, and I am ready to be back there."

" I tell you what, I'll go check with the nurse to see if we can get an answer one way or another."

" You don't need to go to any trouble. I'm sure they'll let me know here soon." Mathew loved her for caring.

" It's no trouble at all. Besides, I need to know, so I can make sure I have the right supplies, if I have to bust you out. I'm not normally a law breaker, but for you, I think I can come up with some sort of plan to sneak you out of here, if they're unwilling to let you go. Not that I would blame them. I wouldn't want to let you go either, as you sure brighten the day." Faith gave him a sweet smile.

Mathew shook his head with a smile. " Now who's head is going to be too big to fit through the doorway?"

" Don't worry; I was told the doors are oversized to accommodate wheel chairs." Faith chuckled. Then headed out to see if she could get someone that might know if he was going to be able to go home today or not. She hoped he would be, as she knew he really was ready to go home.

It didn't take Faith long to find a nurse, who said she'd try to find out, and would let them know as soon as she could. Faith thanked her, and went back to the room to wait, and visit with Mathew.

" I spoke with a nurse, who will try to find out if you'll be released today. She'll let us know as soon as she finds out." Faith said as she was sitting down next to the bed.

" Thank you Faith. I truly appreciate you going to ask. It would be good to sleep in my own bed, under my own roof tonight." Mathew was very much enjoying his time with Faith, but he was beyond ready to be home. At least there, he would have pictures of his wife to look at. He did hope Faith would still come over and visit regularly. It had been so nice having her company. In fact, he figured he'd miss seeing her everyday, even though it'd only been a few days since she came in his life.

" I can understand that. I do hope to get you back to your home today too. If they're worried about you being alone there, I can and will be able to be there to help you with whatever you might need." Faith assured him, just like she did the nurse.

" You don't have to do that. You have your own life to get back to. You do not have to worry about me Faith. You own me nothing." Mathew didn't want her to feel like she had to be there to take care of him.

" It's not about owing you Mr. Gospel. It's about wanting to help you if I can, and getting to spend more time with you. I've been enjoying our visits more than you know. It's the first time in years that I wanted to sit and visit with anyone. And that means something!" Faith couldn't believe she opened up like that, and said so much. The surprise was written all over her face.

Mathew knew he needed to tread cautiously, or she might close right back up. He figured that just saying what her visits have meant to him would be the best response. " These visits have meant a lot to me as well, Fatih. I don't want to lose them either. I hope my going home doesn't change us getting together and visiting regularly." Mathew was hoping to continue seeing Faith regularly, and decided there would be no harm in voicing that to her. He hoped it made Faith feel more at ease, as well. He wanted her to stay comfortable and open up more, and talk about herself, and that pain in her eyes.

If Mathew would want to do one more important thing in this world before his time ran out, it would be to help Faith.

" Really?" Faith was beyond surprised to hear him say that.

" Truly. Will you do me the honor and pleasure of continuing our visits when I'm out of here?" He asked her formally, so there would be no misunderstandings.

Faith got tears in her eyes. Happy tears, which she couldn't ever remembering having.

" It would be my greatest honor." Faith replied.

Mathew reached out for her with both arms. Faith didn't hesitate, she leaned in, and accepted his hug. It felt familiar, and comfortable. Two feelings she hadn't had since the passing of her mother.

They didn't get to speak right away after the hug, as the nurse came in to give them an update.

" Mr. Gospel, I'm sorry to say we are going to miss you, since you get to go home today." The nurse said with a smile at the end.

" I have to say that is music to my ears! Thank you all for taking such wonderful care of me. God bless you, and your healing hands." Mathew was relieved to hear he was going home.

" It's been a pleasure. I have a few things to go over for you to continue your care at home. Then we will get the paperwork in order, so you can head home, before lunch."

The nurse went over everything with both Mathew and Faith.

About an hour later Faith was pulling her SUV around to pick up Mathew at the front doors of the hospital.

Faith input Mathew's address into her GPS, so she could just let Mathew rest and not have to worry about navigating her through the busy streets. Faith wondered if the streets ever stopped being so busy. It never seemed to matter the time of the day, traffic was always bad.

Mathew started talking about a more simple time, and when the streets were never this busy. There weren't as many buildings either, back then he explained, stores, and houses had trees out front, as well as in the back yards. The air was more refreshing also back then. Said it still smelled like nature when you went for a walk.

Faith was enjoying hearing him describe it. It seemed like it would certainly be far better then what it is today. She mentally shook her head at " progress." It seems progress was just the world's word for more expensive living, and less enjoyable. In other words now progress seemed to equal greed.

Faith knew this wasn't the best way to feel or think about things, but the experiences in her life didn't allow for her to view it any other way. It was sad.

" Has spending so much time with me a burden to you Faith?" Mathew asked as she looked tired. She looked tired from the first day he had met her, so he wasn't sure if it was due to spending extra time with him, or just the daily struggles of life. Mathew noticed many people looked more worn down now days.

" Oh, not at all! Spending time with you has been just wonderful. I look forward to it everyday. It's been such an enjoyable part within my day, and life!" Faith was surprised by his sudden question. She wasn't expecting it.

" I'm happy to hear that. It's been giving me great joy. I look forward to our visits everyday, as well. Visiting with you is doing this old man's heart good. It feels good to get to share my stories. Without having any children or grandchildren, I've never been able to pass them down. You honor me, by allowing me to share them with you, young lady." Mathew never thought about it before, but getting to share them with her made him realize how important it was to him.

" Trust me when I say this; the honor and pleasure is all mine! It's been too long since I've looked forward to much, of anything in life, or enjoyed just visiting with another for that matter." Faith wanted him to know she was getting so much from their time together, and it was in no way a burden.

It didn't take them very long to get to Mathew's home. Faith didn't know why, and couldn't understand it, but Mathew's home felt comfortable and like home to her from the minute she walked inside. Faith hadn't had that feeling of coming home since before her mother passed away. Even her own apartment never felt comfortable or like home to her. There were so much that had been bringing up feelings, that Faith hadn't had for many years, since meeting Mathew. It didn't make any sense to her, but yet she didn't want to walk away, and lose those feelings either. That in itself was mind blowing to her. She worked hard to avoid any meaningful connections, because meaningful connections were far too painful. She never wanted to feel that pain again.

When Faith loss her mother, she lost a big part of herself, and she never gained that part back. She worked hard to keep that part of herself closed off to everyone. Yet she wasn't fighting to keep it closed off with Mathew.

Mathew showed Faith around the house as they walked to the kitchen, as Mathew really wanted a cup of tea.

" Crazy thing is I never really enjoyed tea, but it was something Lovey, loved. She said we were going to make it a point to have a tea time together each and everyday. She refused to let life get too busy. It wasn't about the tea, it was just a time to make sure we sat down and really connected, and listened to each other. Now that she's gone, I still have my tea time. At first I thought it was out of habit, but then I realized it was to honor each time I sat here with her. Keeping her love and memories present in my mind, heart, and day."

" That's really beautiful Mr. Gospel; I never considered those things could be a way to honor those gone." Faith said with honesty.

Mathew was surprised by Faith's response, but now he knew from where the pain within her was coming, in some way. He just didn't know who she lost or how long ago it was.

" I don't know if others see it that way or not, but I know I was given such a wonderful gift; getting to share my life with Lovey, and I want to honor that gift, even though she is no longer here. Her passing didn't make the gift any less amazing, and wonderful, and I don't want it to seem that way. If that makes any sense."

" It does. It actually makes complete sense. I wish I was told that years ago. It might have helped me." Faith abruptly stopped talking. She couldn't believe she said that.

Mathew gave her a moment to see if she wanted to say more, but when it was clear she didn't he again, didn't push. He knew she'd open up when she was ready. Seemed like her heart was opening up and things were slipping out, rather she wanted them to or not.

He wondered if this is what it would have felt like having a child or grandchild? Maybe Lovey, and God sent Fatih to him to give him just one more priceless gift. Love in any form is a truly priceless gift.

Mathew would be the first person to say that he lacked for nothing in his lifetime, in fact he'd tell you he had an abundance of love. Yet somehow suddenly having Faith in his life, it felt like a new part he never had in his heart, opened up to make room for Faith to be able to fill.

It's a wondrous miracle how a heart can suddenly have more room, when you already felt like it was overflowing with love. A true God given gift! Mathew thought it especially special with Christmas right around the corner. It is the season for miracles after all. He could almost hear those words in Lovey's voice, as she spoke them many times through the years.

" Are you getting hungry Faith? I don't have much in the cupboards, but I think we can come up with something." Mathew didn't even consider she would want to leave right away.

" I am getting a little hungry, but how about I come up with something, while you sit and keep me company? You really should take it easy yet. Besides, I'm ready for the next story you are willing to share with me." Faith gave him a reassuring smile.

" I can agree to those terms." Mathew smiled back at her.

Again, Faith found herself completely at ease, even going through the cupboards to find something to make them for lunch. She would have sworn she would never be this comfortable at anyone's home, especially of someone she just met. Yet, the fact is she is completely comfortable.

Time seemed to fly by as it always does. They had a lovely lunch with an even better story. After they finished lunch Faith got Mathew settled in the living room, as that's where he wanted to settle in for a little rest.

Faith decided to run a couple of errands, and let Mathew just rest without having to worry about entertaining her. She promised to be back in a couple of hours, but told him to call her cellphone if he needed her before that.

Mathew offered her a house key, so she didn't have to worry about waiting to make sure he was a wake before trying to come back into the house Faith didn't argue, and accepted the key, as it did make the most sense.

Mathew found himself smiling as she headed out. He was feeling the presence of his dear wife in this " chance meeting." He said to the heavens, a special thank you to his wife, and to God. Mathew knew his life was very blessed, with all the love and time he had with Lovey, so this extra gift was quite a surprise, and an even bigger blessing. An unexpected one, which his wife always said are the very best kind.

He fell asleep with a smile on his face, and an abundance of love in his heart.

Faith's first stop was to her apartment to grab a few things, as she planned on staying with Mr. Gospel, if it was all right with him, at least for the first night. Then she went to pick up some groceries, so she'd have everything to make meals for the next few days. After she had all the errands finished, she went back to the house, and quietly let herself back inside. She found Mathew still sleeping, so she just went to the kitchen and took care of everything. Once everything was taken care of properly, she opened her computer to get some work done.

That's exactly where Mathew found her when he got up a couple hours later.

" I didn't realize you were back. I have to say, I'm very happy to see you sitting here." Mathew had a slight smile.

" You seemed to be sleeping so well, that I decided to just do some work in here, and not disturb you." Faith was happy he seemed to be moving around well.

" Don't let me keep you from your work. I just had an urge for a cup of tea." Mathew knew that was due to feeling the presence of his wife, and was so grateful for it.

" I've actually gotten more done in the last two hours than I normally do, so I can certainly take a break. I'm ahead of schedule. Would you mind me joining you for that cup of tea?"

" I would be honored." Mathew said meaning it whole heartedly.

After they had their cups of tea, and were sitting at the table together Faith decided it was a good time to ask him for a favor.

" May I ask you a favor Mr. Gospel?"

" Of course, but please call me Mathew." He asked her again.

" Ok, I'll try. I would appreciate it if you would allow me to stay here just tonight. I wouldn't feel right leaving you here alone, your first night out of the hospital." Faith hoped he would agree. She didn't want to make him feel like she was intruding.

" I'm sure I'll be just fine, but I'm wise enough to not turn down your kind offer. It'll be nice to have another person here to help bring this house to life in the morning as well. Lovey always said it took love and joy to bring the house to life in the mornings."

" Your wife was a very wise woman, with a very loving and unique way about her, from what I've heard about her already." Faith smiled almost feeling like she had known her when she was alive.

" She certainly was. She wasn't perfect, but those little flaws made us fit together all the better. No one on earth is perfect, but I think that's part of the big picture; so we can find our person, and know it without a doubt, as we fit together perfectly. Like a puzzle, we fit together perfectly to make a full and complete picture, that is our lives." Mathew had a wistful smile, remembering how perfectly they had fit.

" I'm learning so many wonderful, and new ways to look at and see things in life, from you. You are a true gift in my life Mathew. I want you to know how grateful I am to have met you, and to have this time with you." Faith said full of emotion.

" How about we make a deal? We both keep making sure to say how happy and grateful we are to have this time together, so why don't we just accept this means a lot to both of us, and not feel like we need to keep saying it so much?" Mathew wanted her to know that he knows how she feels, and they could just visit.

" I can agree with that." Faith smiled, knowing exactly what he meant. They were both thrown by this surprising gift, but it was time to focus on their time together and not worry so much about the rest.

" Good, as can I. It is always good to express gratitude, but I feel like we've gotten that all covered." Mathew smiled in return.

" I never knew my grandparents, but I think this is what it would have been like if I did get to know them. With them sharing the stories of their lives. At least, that's what I would have asked to hear them talk about, if I could have. I enjoy hearing the stories of people who lived in less technological times. Even though my job is on the computer, I think life had a different way, that was more simple in some ways back then."

" You're not wrong. In a lot of ways things were more simple. Yet other things weren't as good. Medical advances have been good to a point, as have equipment for working, and other things like that. However somethings have gone too far, beyond advances that were good, to making some things worse. All these self checkouts for example have replaced good old fashion customer service. Just as this world of abundance has destroyed the value of things. People have so much and no longer see how blessed they are to have all they do."

" I went to college with people who wanted the newest this or that, so would get it, and just throw away the older versions. This line of thought, is something I could never understand. It just seems so wasteful. It's like no one ever considers this is the only world we have, and it's getting covered with waste and garbage."

" Lovey said the same thing, as we saw that way of living becoming the normal. It broke her heart. She started volunteering at places that would find new homes of these useful things yet, and try to encourage donation over throwing things away. It became part of her mission." Mathew said with pride laced in his words. He was always so proud of the work she did, to try to make the world a better place.

" Well, that was a worthy mission to work towards. I think I would have really liked your wife, just like I do you." Faith said with such sincerity.

" I know she would have adored you, young lady. I know I certainly do." Mathew replied with the same sincerity.

They sat in a comfortable silence as they sipped their tea. Both lost in their own thoughts.

Mathew thinking about his Lovey, and how he knew she had a hand in Faith coming into his life. Fatih thinking about her mother, and allowing herself to remember their life together, for the first time in years.

" Faith, are you all right?" Mathew noticed tears developing in her eyes.

" Oh yes, I'm sorry. I was just thinking about my mom." Words Faith had never spoken to another.

Mathew reached across the table and took her hand in comfort. He felt like he could ask a little now, so he gently asked, " When did you lose her?" There was no denying that hurt in her eyes, so he knew she had indeed lost her mother.

" A long time ago. It was a few months away from my 18th birthday. It was around the Christmas season. I've been annoyed by all things Christmas ever since. That's how I ended up crashing into you at the store. I was angry to be unable to avoid the Christmas items, and that they were out already."

" I am sorry you lost her so young, and at that time of year, as well. It couldn't have been easy, but it can't be easy carrying annoyance over Christmas all these years either." Mathew was blunt, yet compassionate.

It turned out to be exactly what Faith needed. She let his words sink in before speaking again. " I never realized it before, but you're right. It hasn't been. I think it kept me from remembering the good times, and memories of my mom. The day we met was the first time I had any memories come to mind, since not long after I lost her. Today has also been the first time I've gone into a store and didn't get angry about the Christmas items out on display. I somehow feel lighter." Faith was a bit confused how all that happened so suddenly, and grateful to not have that constant feeling of tightness in her chest. That feeling had been with her since her mother first got sick. She had forgotten what it felt like to not have it. Suddenly breathing didn't require as much effort.

" I can understand that. The weight of anger holds our souls down, and doesn't let love lift us back up when we need it the most. I'm glad you are able to start shedding that weight. I will pray it continues, and you can stay free from it." Mathew wasn't surprised to suddenly have the exact words to say, as he knew God put them there, just for Faith in this moment.

" Thank you." Faith was unashamed when a few tears flowed freely down her cheeks.

Mathew just continued to hold her hand in comfort, and silently bowed his head in prayer for her right then and there.

After he finished his prayer he looked into Faith's eyes to gauge if he should ask any more questions, or just change the topic for now.

" Would you like to share more now, or do you need time to sit with this for a while?" Mathew asked with such care and compassion, as he couldn't tell from just looking at her.

" I think I could use some time, if you don't mind. I'm feeling a little overwhelmed, yet it's ok as I can remember my mom right now, without all the anger." What Faith didn't share was the tightness in her throat as the grief was hitting her.

" That's more than all right. I think it's a wise choice, to just take the time to allow those thoughts and feelings to come as they may. Allowing yourself time to deal with them is a good thing to do."

" I would love to share more later, though." Faith did say. She wanted him to know she was comfortable enough with him to share, after she had time to deal, just as he said.

" I'm here to listen whenever you're ready." He gave her a smile, and also gave her hand another gentle squeeze before releasing it.

They sat in silence as they finished the tea.

" Do you play cards at all Faith?" Mathew asked after their tea was finished.

" I haven't played in a very long time, but I would love to play a game. You might have to teach me how to play, but I'm usually a quick study, and pick up things quickly." Faith thought this will be so fun, and her smile matched her thought.

" Have you ever play cribbage?" Mathew and his wife used to play it all the time.

" No, but I always wanted to learn how to play. It always looked so interesting and fun." Faith was excited to get to learn how to play it finally.

Mathew got the cards and board out, and spent time explaining the rules and how to play. He even pulled out example hands for them to play out together.

Faith couldn't believe how wonderful Mathew was at explaining the rules and how to play. By the time they started playing, she felt confident that she knew what she was doing.

They spent the rest of the afternoon playing cribbage. Then they cooked dinner together, as Mathew refused to allow her to cook alone again.

After they cleaned up from dinner, they decided on a movie to watch.

Mathew thanked God again that night for bringing Faith into his life. Faith too prayed that night. She hadn't prayed since the day before her mother passed away. She thanked God for sending Mathew to help her find her way, and promised to not lose her way again. Then she slept better than she had since before her mom had gotten sick.

Faith stayed there so she could be there if Mathew needed her, but it was Mathew who checked in on her durning the night.

Chapter Four

Much to Faith's surprise she had slept soundly, and woke up feeling hopeful and refreshed. She found Mathew in the kitchen already heating tea water.

" I thought I was supposed to be here to help you?" Faith said with a smile.

" Having you here last night helped heal my lonely heart, Fatih." He replied with a smile as well. " How'd you sleep?"

" I'm almost ashamed to admit that I didn't wake up once. I slept soundly. I hope you didn't need me through the night. I usually never sleep that soundly, or through the night." Faith admitted.

" I'm very happy to hear that you slept so well. I didn't need you through the night, so don't feel ashamed. Sounds like you needed a good nights sleep."

Faith suddenly realized that she had to leave today. It was clear that he didn't need her there, to help him.

It must have shown all over her face as Mathew asked, " What's wrong?"

" It's pretty silly, but I'm sad knowing I have to go back to my place today. I know we just met, but it feels like I'm with family again, like it was when I was still with my mom." With that being said a single tear slipped silently down her cheek.

Mathew's heart melted. He opened up his arms to hug her. She didn't hesitate. She accepted his hug.

" Oh Faith, you feel like family to me too dear. You feel like the granddaughter we never had. You certainly don't have to go anywhere. It's given my heart such joy having you in my life, and here with me. It was the best accident, I have ever had in my life. I have been dreading you leaving today too. I'm not too proud to say, I've been fearing you walking out that door and out of my life."

Faith smiled at him after the hug ended. " That means I don't have to leave, and when I do, I'm welcomed to come back?" Faith wanted to make sure she didn't misunderstand him.

" I'd be heartbroken if you didn't stay in my life." He assured her.

" That's settled then, you are stuck with me! Would it be all right if I called you grandpa? A name of honor, because you feel like what I always thought having a grandfather would feel like."

This time it was Mathew who was getting tears in his eyes. It took him a few moments to gather his emotions, before he could speak. " It would be one of the biggest honors of my life." He said with the love he felt in each word.

With that Faith leaned in and gave him a kiss on his cheek. Then smiled with nothing but love before saying, " Good morning grandpa!"

Mathew chuckled with pure joy and love. " Good morning granddaughter!"

" Well, what are we going to have for breakfast. I'm pretty handy around the kitchen, so what do you feel like having this morning."

" Normally, I wouldn't ask this of just anyone, but I know my granddaughter won't mind; how about an omelet with bacon and cheese?" Mathew was grinning getting to call her his granddaughter again.

" I can do that. How about some toast and potatoes on the side too?" Faith offered.

" Yes, please! That sounds perfect! I'm finding myself rather hungry this morning."

" Then I'll get right at it!" That was when Faith realized she had found the joy within her heart again. She thought she was happy, but it was in that moment when she knew she hadn't had true joy.

Faith never thought happiness and joyfulness were two different things. Happiness was good, but it was fleeting. Joy was something much deeper within yourself. It wasn't something anyone could change. It was something much more profound, and had a deeper meaning.

Letting Mathew into her life, opened a door that she had shut years ago. The day she shut that door, was the day she lost any possibility of having true joy in her life.

Faith had thought that shutting that door was protecting her from more hurt, but all it really did was stop her from having and feeling the love and joy God was always sending her way.

The minute she allowed Mathew into her life and heart, she reopened that door, and she could feel God's love fill her very being.

Faith stopped gathering the items to make breakfast, to bow her head right then and there to pray:

"Father I come to you first to apologize for letting my hurt cause me to deny Your love. I did not realize what I was doing, but now I see the truth of what I did, and how much I was missing.

Thank You Father for not giving up on me, and for sending me the love only You can. My heart is open again, and I can feel Your presence again. I thought I was still honoring You, but I know I was not. I will do better Father! I will never deny Your love, and the joy and peace that comes from knowing it. I will do better to honor You Father and I will keep my heart open, so I never deny You or Your love again. All honor and praise to You. Amen"

Mathew sat silently watching her, and knew she was speaking with God. That's when he knew the reason they were brought together. Faith needed to find a safe place and someone to help her find her way back to God. He was happy she had found her way back, yet he was grateful that she helped him find joy in his life again as well.

He had forgotten the simple joy in those quiet moments with God. He prayed everyday, but it was out of habit, he now realized. Now he prayed again for the joy of it, and to feel closer to God. Mathew said a silent, " Thank You, Father," as well.

He smiled into his tea and thought of Lovey, and what she'd be saying about all of this. "Divine Intervention," is what she'd say. God always works in the best ways. Bringing people together to help each other with whatever they needed the most. God always knows what we need even if we don't. That's when Divine Intervention happens: to give each person the guidance to find what they need.

She had said that sometimes life, and evil can overwhelm us, and we stop hearing God, or feeling His endless love. That's when God would send someone that also needed help too. There are times that we are the tools for God's work. The key that unlocks the blockage; and opens the doorway to God back up.

Matthew knew Lovey was certainly right now, about all of that. He also felt mighty grateful that God intervened, and sent

Faith to help him find the key to unlock the door to his heart again.

Mathew remembered back, and smiled. That's the second time God sent faith to me through another person. He couldn't be more grateful for both of them. God does work in wondrous ways.

Both Mathew and Faith were silent while she made breakfast, both lost in forgotten joy and love. Neither willing to stop embracing it just yet.

After breakfast was prepared, and on the table, they joined hands, to give thanks, before sharing the lovely meal.

" This is very good. Thank you. I was craving an omelet for sometime now." Mathew said between bites.

" It was my pleasure. I forgot about the enjoyment I get from cooking for another person. Funny how much I'm against change, yet I stopped doing so many of the things I enjoyed, after my mom passed, and caused even more unnecessary changes." Faith replied with a shake of her head.

" Even at my old age, change is hard. Makes you wonder why, when the only constant, besides God, in our lives since birth is change. Maybe the lesson is that we should embrace the changes and the growth that can come from them?"

Faith thought for a second before responding. " I've never thought of it that way. Yet it seems like it is exactly the way it is."

" Honestly, it's the first time I thought of it that way myself. Funny how sometimes things hit us out of the blue."

" Maybe that should be our goal everyday for now on; to embrace changes, and try to grow with them. Instead of fighting them, and clinging to what's familiar. Maybe that's part, of the key, to having a joyful life here." Faith said thoughtfully.

" I love that!" Mathew replied with excitement. " Let's do it! I'll try to help you, and you try to help me when change hits. We'll try to embrace it with grace and trust, and grow with it."

" All right, sounds like a great plan. It might actually be fun. I'm sure it's not going to be easy; breaking a lifelong habit of fighting change, but I think it's certainly a worthy goal." Faith nodded her head.

" Definitely." Mathew agreed. He was surprisingly excited to try to embrace the changes that come his way.

" You realize grandpa, that we've already started embracing change, when we met." Faith said somewhat shocked with the realization.

" Well, my goodness, you're right, we did! I guess the good Lord wanted us to continue this new adventure of just embracing changes. I'm sure that's why I was given that thought out of the blue." Mathew couldn't help but to smile at the amazing miracles God gave him, this week alone. Not to mention all the many other miracles he's witnessed durning his lifetime so far.

" Kind of making me look forward to change, for the first time ever!" Faith was both in aww and excited. The Lord is great, she thought.

" Me too!" Mathew said. He knew all changes wouldn't be as easy as adding Faith into his life, but he figured if God made them happen, it was for a purpose that played into the bigger picture that only God can see.

They enjoyed their breakfast together, where Faith told Mathew more about her job, when he asked about it.

She found it refreshing to sit and talk about her work with someone. Seemed like such a small thing, yet it was a huge thing to her. Faith never considered that such a small thing like talking about her work would feel like a big deal. Then it made sense. It wasn't just talking about her work; it was being willing to share her life with another person.

Mathew was like a grandfather, so it wasn't about sharing her life with a romantic partner, but sharing her life with someone she trusted and respected. Love in any form made life all the better.

" Could you imagine going through life without knowing God, or His love, grandpa?"

" Thank God, no. I couldn't even imagine such a horrible thing. This world is so hard at times, and evil is always lurking. I don't know how anyone could survive without God's love. What made you ask that?"

" I was thinking about how much sharing even the small aspect of my work life made me feel. It made me realize how much love, in any form, really makes a difference."

" Love does make all the difference. Keeping love in your heart, and choosing to lead with love as your guide always, makes life's struggles just a little bit easier to get through. That love stops them from overwhelming you. It keeps you out of the darkness. It shields you from evil. Evil will never stop trying to pull us into the darkness; it's having that love within our hearts that makes sure we are never lost in darkness. That light is within all of us. The more we let it lead us, the brighter it shines. The less darkness is in our lives, thus the less evil has a chance to lurk in it, and invade our lives."

"There's more power in love than we tend to give it. Isn't there, grandpa?" Faith smile every time she called him grandpa. It felt so right, and so wonderful; having family again.

"I think even more than we'll ever know, until we go home to Father in heaven." Mathew's heart melted more, with each time she called him grandpa. What was more shocking was how right it felt to him. Fatih felt so much like family, just as much as his wife did. He felt like Faith was a true granddaughter. Another lesson he learned since meeting her: Family didn't have to be blood. Funny how we marry people to become family, yet we never think that we can accept others as family in other ways like this, he thought. Connection and love can make anyone our family, if we allow it.

Mathew felt a little odd just now learning these things, at his age. However it was suddenly clear that only we can put limits on love and family.

They did up the dishes together and decided on lunch and dinner. Then Mathew decided on some reading time, so Faith could just focus on her work for a while, as he didn't want to make her get behind on her work.

It was a very nice morning, just being in the same house. Even though they were doing their own things, it made them both feel more content.

Faith had always been a hard worker, and never had issues with getting her work done on time, and with high quality. Yet today she took actual joy in her work, and somehow that made a huge difference, as she managed to get half a weeks worth of work done just that morning, and early afternoon. She usually was ahead of the deadlines, but not as much as was now.

She was really surprised. She had thought she always enjoyed her work, but without having a truly joyful heart, it, like everything in her life, lacked. She looked at her work calendar, thinking maybe she could take a little time off, and just explore this new found joy in her life.

Looking at the calendar gave her an amazingly wonderful idea. She went ahead and sent the email that she'd be taking time off between November 20th thru November 26th. She stated that she'd have all the work on her calendar completed up to the 20th, before she was off for that week. She felt such satisfaction hitting the send box. Then she decided it was time for lunch, and time to ask Mathew if he'd help her with her plan for that week she now has off from work.

" Hey, grandpa, are you ready for some lunch? I was getting a bit hungry, and was surprised to see the time." Faith leaned down to kiss his cheek.

Mathew smiled. " I am a bit hungry myself. I nodded off for a bit, and just started reading again a little while ago." He was moved by her small gesture of love; that little kiss on the cheek.

Mathew had never felt like his life had missed out on anything. Even though he and his wife were unable to have any children, he felt his life had always been complete and lacked for nothing. Yet he had to admit that having Faith, a granddaughter, filled his heart, in a way he would have never imagined. He was grateful for such an unexpected gift.

Mathew always knew and believed God took care of all His children, but it wasn't until God brought Faith into his life, that Mathew knew God always gave them everything they needed, even if His children didn't know they needed what they were given.

They made up a simple lunch together. Then sat down and gave grace, before starting to eat. They chatted about the book Mathew was reading, and about Faith's work she'd done that morning. It was a perfectly lovely meal shared with each other.

After they finished eating Faith did up the dishes, while Mathew got at preparing them both a cup of tea. When they sat down to enjoy their tea, Faith brought up her idea.

" Grandpa, do you have plans for Thanksgiving?"

" Sadly, I'll be spending it here alone. How about you? Do you go to friends? What do they call that, Friendsgiving?"

" That is what they call it, but no. I've never gone to anything like that. To be completely honest, I usually stay home trying to ignore the holidays all together. However, this year I'm hoping to do things very differently, embracing change. Do you think you can help me with that?" Faith gave him a small smile. Hoping he'd be agreeable to her plan, yet not wanting to make him feel pressured.

" You name it kiddo, I'll do whatever I can to help change that tradition of yours." Mathew was hoping that meant she'd be spending Thanksgiving with him.

" Perfect! We better start planning *Our* Thanksgiving meal, before everything sells out." Faith went to grab a pen and paper. Knowing that they'd be spending the day together.

Mathew lowered his head to give thanks. " Thank You, Father, for giving me another chance at family. It's certainly not what I expected; a granddaughter to come into my life, yet I cannot thank You more Father. I will cherish this very special gift. All Honor and Praise to You. Amen."

Faith had come back into the kitchen and saw Mathew had his head bowed down, and she figured he was praying. She stood silently, so she didn't interrupt him.

When Mathew raised his head, and opened his eyes, he was surprised to see Faith just standing there, silently with her head bowed out of respect, as her eyes were open. He figured she was just honoring his prayer. His eyes filled with tears of pure love, joy, and gratitude.

" Come on in. I'm done saying my prayer. Thank you for waiting for me to finish. It was very thoughtful of you."

" It's not a big deal. Just something my mother told me about always be respectful, especially when someone is feeling the need to speak with God."

" Your mother must have been a very thoughtful woman." Mathew said, wishing he could have known her.

" She was. I remember her stopping many times throughout the day to give thanks, or ask for guidance when she was struggling. I hadn't thought of that for years. Walking in and seeing you in prayer brought those memories to mind. I think this is the first time memories of her didn't make me feel like I was going to break, with the hurt of losing her. I think that's due to you." Faith reached her hand out for his as she sat down, at the table with him.

" I was just thanking God for you." Mathew said as he took her hand in his. " My life was very complete with Lovey, and I never felt like we missed out on anything. However I'm finding myself extremely grateful for this blessing of you, my granddaughter."

" I've been missing out of a lot in life, since my mother passed away. I'm now realizing I basically stopped living as well.

I blocked out everything. I went to college, got my degree, and have my career, but in all truth, I didn't really live during all of that time. I never let anyone be close to me. I never let myself be close to anyone. Running into you at the store, scared me so much. I was terrified that I seriously hurt you, and it made me realize I was not doing things correctly. It was talking with you that made me see what I was doing wrong, and this time with you has not just opened my eyes, but changed my life. I feel like I have family again, which I haven't felt like since my mother passed, and I look forward to each day. It's for all of that, that I'm most grateful. Grandpa you opened my heart again."

They sat silent for a moment just getting their emotions in order, yet making sure to feel and honor those feelings, for the gifts they are.

They planned their Thanksgiving feast as they sipped their tea. It was a new experience for them both, as neither of them had ever planned such a meal. It was funny how excited they were both getting about all the work ahead of them, which they both planned on doing together.

Since Mathew was feeling back to normal, he decided to go shopping with Faith for all they'll need. They even discussed the fact that they'd pick up enough for serving 20 or so people, and donate the extras to those in need. They both saw many homeless people, who they could drop the extras off to, so they could have a thanksgiving meal too.

After the meal was planned they just visited about things they wished they could do to help others. Together, they figured, why couldn't they do something? It didn't have to be huge things, even a small thing for one person here and there would be enough of a start.

Mathew said Lovey always said change starts with one small act of kindness. That's when they developed their plans. They even gave it a mission statement, and a tentative name.

Faith was a business genius and made up plans with projected figures, so they had basically made up a full business plan. Mathew was impressed, and started thinking on a plan of his own. He knew he had limited time left; he'd already lived a long and full life, but he wanted to leave the world a better place, with his small act of kindness. Just as Lovey did. She had secretly planned a small act of kindness to be done after she had passed: A donation made in God's name to a homeless shelter.

Mathew had been thinking on his small act to be done in God's name at his passing, before Faith came into his life, he was at a complete loss at what he wanted to do, and had almost given up trying to think of something. Now however Mathew knew exactly what he wanted to do, and he was excited to get everything in place for it. He thought just maybe they could start sooner than his passing.

Faith was excited too, because with their plan she might be able to truly give back in this world, and in the correct ways. She'd always wanted to give to charities, but sadly the world had become so corrupted, and most of the donations went to paychecks more than to those in need, so she didn't give. Now that her and Mathew had this plan, she could. She felt like her mom was looking down and smiling with love and pride. That made Faith feel truly connected to her mother, for the first time in years. Something she thought she'd never feel again, but it was like she could almost feel her mother's embrace, and hear her saying she loved her.

Faith was smiling but the tears were flowing freely. Felt strange feeling joy, love, and grief all at the same time.

Mathew saw her and without saying a word got up and moved over to sit by her. He wrapped his arm around her. Faith didn't say a word, but leaned into his embrace, and just allowed the tears and feelings to come. Mathew didn't try to say anything, but just sat with her for support, as she opened herself up to all those feelings she'd blocked for far too many years.

After a while Faith felt better, and was only feeling the love and joy. " Thank you grandpa. I don't know where all that came from all at once."

" Any time my sweet granddaughter. I'm guessing it's like you said, you blocked out so much for so long, that now that you've opened your heart to life again, everything hit you at once. All those things you've been denying yourself to feel, both good and the harder things too. Are you feeling better now?"

" I am. In a way, I feel lighter of mind and heart. I've had this heavy feeling for so long, I forgot what it was like to not have it. I can't really explain it more than I did the other day."

" You let the light back into your heart and it removed that darkness that was weighing you down." Mathew said as a possible explanation.

" Wow! How did you describe it so perfectly?"

" When my wife passed away, I felt that same way. Then one day something made me just feel her here with me, and I'm guessing I had that very same look on my face when it all hit me. Her love, God's love, joy and the grief of losing her. I broke down just as you did. It was after that when I realized I was crying with the joy of letting God's love ignite within me once again, as much as I was with the grief. Denying myself from feeling the grief, also denied me from letting God's love ignite within my soul, and it gave me the overwhelming feeling of heaviness within my mind and heart. Grief is a part of life. God know's our sorrow, but He tries to help replace it with His light and love. We just have to let Him."

" I feel a little overwhelmed, yet like I just woke up after years of sleepwalking through my life." Faith added.

" Probably the best description of that: Walking in this world without our Heavenly Father is much like that; just going through the motions, yet not feeling the joy, and love behind them." Mathew smile at her as he saw the pain he first noticed surrounding her was no longer there. He knew she still had to fully finishing grieving, but now he knew she would, and she'd feel much better afterwards.

" I couldn't have gotten here without you grandpa. Thank you for helping guide my heart back open, so I can feel the love and joy again."

" Oh sweetheart, I think I had very little to do with bringing you into my life, but I can say it's where you do belong. God intervenes when we need it the most, that's exactly why my wife always called it, "Divine Intervention." A gift and a blessing sent directly from God."

" Will you pray with me? I think I need to speak with God and thank Him, but also to again apologize for blocking His love and guidance for so very long." Faith asked. She was so overwhelmed that his comment about Divine Intervention didn't register and remind her of the time her mom told her about Divine Timing.

" It'd be a honor to share this time in prayer with you. I have my own thanks to give as well." Mathew took Faith's hand as they bowed their heads together in prayer.

They said their prayers in silence, straight from their hearts, and with the gratitude they felt. Without words to each other, they both knew when each other was done, and ended their prayers together with both saying Amen out loud at the same time.

They decided on a relaxing rest of the day. Faith didn't feel the need to ask to stay there again, even though she knew Mathew didn't need her there to help him with anything. It was just an unspoken understanding that she was going to stay.

Mathew knew tomorrow they'd talk more, but he was hoping she'd just move in with him, as there was more than enough room, and it felt like this was where she was meant to be. It seemed like it was something meant for the both of them. Like there was far more work to be done together.

Faith went to bed that night feeling wrapped in light, love, and warmth that can only come from God. She made sure to say another prayer of thanks. Then she slept truly peacefully throughout the night.

Mathew felt more at peace as well, and didn't feel the need to check in on Faith this time. He knew she was going to be ok now, which Mathew too gave thanks to God, before a peaceful night as well.

Chapter Five

The next morning started with joy for both Faith and Mathew. They seemed to have a routine down already, and it flowed like a smooth and calm river. They made breakfast together and shared grace, before eating. Then as Faith did clean up, Mathew brewed their cup of tea to share after breakfast, and got the cribbage game all ready to go.

When Faith sat down she couldn't help but to chuckle.

" What's got you laughing?" Mathew's smile was full of joy and love.

" It's like we've been doing this for years, and it's only been two days. It just caught me as amusing, and it made me happy."

" It makes me happy too. I guess this is what having a child or grandchild living with you is like, which brings me to what I wanted to discuss with you this morning. Now I know that you have your own place, and are very capable of taking care of yourself, but I was wondering if you'd honor me with just moving in here with me? This big old house has more than enough room, and it's been such a breath of fresh air having you here. I know it's a big ask, but it'd do my old heart good to see life back in this house again. With it just being me here, it doesn't feel like home, but with you here it has felt like home again." Mathew wasn't sure if she'd be all right with this, but he knew, in his heart, it was the right thing to do. God gave him a granddaughter; a family; and family should be together especially when they've been alone far too long. Mathew knew he didn't have a lot of years left, before he too would go home to God, and he would be honored to pass down this home to her. He hoped that she'd find her soulmate and fill it with once again with love and family.

" I can't believe I'm going to say this, but yes. I will. I have to admit this has felt like home since I first walked in here. I feel like God is telling me that I'm meant to be here. I don't know why yet, but I know it's true all the same." Faith smiled.

" I know why." Mathew said with a smile.

" You do? Why do you think?" Faith didn't have any clue as to what the answer was.

" Because God wants you to remember the love of family, and to let it fill your heart, so you absolutely and truly start to live life. There is so much to love and enjoy in life, and it all starts with an open heart. I'm supposed to help you keep your heart open, and to learn to lead with love always. When you lead with love in all things, that's when you start to honor life and God's love."

Faith stood up and leaned over the table to kiss Mathew's cheek again. " Thank you grandpa! I love you, and will appreciate this gift you're giving me."

" It's a gift for me as well." Mathew said with full conviction. " Another blessing to count each day." He said.

Faith smiled at him knowing she'd be counting it too.

" I'll start making arrangements this week. I will have to go and do some packing, of course, but I think it'd be easiest to hirer movers to do the lifting." Faith just shook her head in awe.

" What's that about? Did you suddenly realize something? Are you still moving in here?" Mathew was surprised by his fear of her not coming home to stay.

" Oh no. I'm still moving home, grandpa!" The excitement and joy was clear to hear and see on her face. " I just realized

God's Divine Intervention was in this too. My lease is up at the end of this month, and I was going to read over the new lease contract to sign it, the day I literally ran into you. I never got to it, thankfully, so it'll be no issues holding up from me moving out of my apartment." Once again the memory of her mother teaching her about Divine Timing didn't come to mind, as her excitement and planning was going through her mind.

Mathew couldn't help it, he started laughing.

" Ok, grandpa, spill! What were you about to do?" Faith could just tell by his laughter he was too on the verge of doing something big, that God had a better plan instead.

" I was going to go by a realtors' office after I finished my shopping to see about selling this place. It was feeling too big and empty for just me. So yes, God indeed intervened to help us both exactly when we needed it most, even though we didn't realize it."

Faith just looked up and simply said, " Thank You. We hear You!"

" Amen to that." Mathew agreed wholeheartedly.

After they finished their tea, and a game of cribbage, they both got ready to head to the store, to get the items for their first family Thanksgiving together. Faith decided to pickup some packing items as well.

She found it amazing that she felt so sure about this move. Every time she had moved in the past, she always felt nervous and unsure. Even with just renewing a lease for a place she was already living, those feelings were there. Her apartment was actually a rather nice place, yet she still never felt at home, and was struggling with those feelings about signing the new lease.

This time there was none of those feelings. It just felt right, and like coming home.

Mathew said they should stop after shopping to at least get some more things, she could use now, and maybe get started on some of the packing. No sense in not taking advantage of the trip there.

Faith agreed it was a good idea. She did need a few more things, until she moved all of her things there. Plus she needed to let her landlord know she was moving, so they could list the apartment for rent, at the end of her existing lease, in a couple of weeks.

Shopping with Mathew was such fun! Faith even stopped and enjoyed the Christmas items on display. That got them talking about Christmas, and what decorating items they had and what items they'd need.

They realized they'd need to make a list, and another shopping trip would be required. Neither of them had much of any Christmas decorations, since they hadn't done a full Christmas in years. Even Mathew had cut back on Christmas decorating before his wife passed, as it was too much for them to do on their own. Going all out again for Christmas had them both excited to do some decoration shopping.

Together they seemed to have started living, with the help of God. They found a family within each other, with God at the center of it.

Even Mathew, who thought he'd lived out his life, without feeling it lacked, realized God had given him more love in this life to share with her. God gave Mathew a new family in a different form, but still with a lot of love.

Faith, who had lived her life alone, without family for far too long, found love in the form of a grandfather, and it reconnected the broken pieces of her life. God found a way to open her heart to love, and all the joyous gifts that came with it.

Neither of them wondered what the future would bring, and what other blessings God would gift them with. They just cherished all that God had blessed them with, and appreciated each moment it gave them.

This gift of each other, of a family, was enough and more than either of them thought was possible. It taught them that God works in the best ways. Theirs was not to question, but theirs to cherish, enjoy, and love.

Two very different generations, with different lives, yet both needing this blessing, and lesson in life and love.

They both knew somewhere in heaven God, Mathew's wife, and Faith's mother were all smiling down at them. Happy and relieved that they both listened to God's guidance, when He brought them together. Love in any form matters in everyone's life. It's all a form created from God's own love. It'a a gift God gives us here on earth to help remind us all of the love He has for each and every one of His children. That's why love is called the greatest gift.

Love has the power to change a life, and the world. God will find ways to show us that, when we need it the most: Divine Intervention!

They got everything they needed for Thanksgiving dinner, and some packing items to get Faith started. After a small argument on who was going to pay, which Faith won. They were on their way to her apartment, and the next chapter of their lives.

Mathew had picked his vehicle back up from the parking lot, and was just following Faith to her apartment. He knew he could have just headed back home with the groceries, which they put into his vehicle, to leave hers free for some of the things she wanted to bring back today, but it felt right to go in, to help her with what packing he could.

Faith got him settled then went to the landlord's office, and let them know that she wasn't renewing her lease.

They wished her well, but were sad to see her leave. Faith thought that was weird, as they didn't really talk. Then she realized it was probably because she was quiet, and dependable with rent. She never had people coming and going. She was most likely a tenants dream renter.

When Faith got back to her apartment she found Mathew had a box and a half already packed up.

" Wow! With your help, I'll be packed up in no time at all! Thanks grandpa!"

" You're welcome. I'm just so happy to have you home, anything I can do to help with that, I'm happy to do." Mathew was grinning as he packed up her dishes with care. It also made him extra happy to give her a home, after he saw how limited she had been living.

Material things didn't make a life, but it broke Mathew's heart to not see any photos or what would be cherished items filled with memories. He wanted to give her some of that in her life, so when God took him home, she could have pictures to look at, with the family he knew God would bless her with, to help remind her, of some wonderful times.

They spent the rest of the morning packing. Faith had the idea of ordering in lunch, so they could finish packing up the rest of the items they had boxes enough for, that way she'd have an idea of how many more boxes she'd need to finish the last of the packing.

Mathew agreed, thinking the sooner they had her home, the better.

After lunch, it didn't take them long to finish with what boxes were left. Faith packed up some of her clothing and items she wanted right away, then they started out, to head home.

" Thank you grandpa, for all your help. I should be about to finish packing the rest up tomorrow. I wouldn't have gotten so much done today without your help."

" You're welcome. I'm happy to help. I know these old bones have limits, but it's good to be useful where I can be yet."

" Oh grandfather, you are more useful than just helping me pack! You gave me a new look on, and basically a new life: One with hope, joy, and love. Old bones and all!" Faith winked and smiled. She had to drive home, so she didn't want to get too emotional, so she added the lighthearted comment.

Mathew laughed. " I love you Faith. Thank you for that. For the record, you gave me much of the same."

" I love you too, grandpa." Faith gave him a heartwarming smile and a hug.

They got her needed items loaded in her vehicle, and then headed home. Mathew still followed her back to the house. They had groceries to carry in as well as the little bit Faith brought back today, so they wanted to be home before too late.

Thankfully, traffic was light, as they beat the rush hour. They got home and unloaded before it got dark. If they'd got caught in rush hour traffic, there would have been a good chance of having to unload in the dark. As it got dark so early this time of the year.

Mathew and Faith walked around the house and were figuring out where she could put her things. It was a four bedroom, two bathroom home, and Mathew had two of the bedrooms empty. It took him a couple of years, but he finally was able to let go of the items that were his wife's, and a lot of the extras to those in need.

He wondered at the time the reason to feel the need to empty the two rooms. Now he knew it was all to prepare for Faith to move in here in with him. He was glad it was because of that, and not because he was selling the house.

" You know, we can hire someone to add an adjoining door here, so you can have your bedroom area in one side, and a sitting/office work area in the other. I'd be happy to call a wonderful contractor I know to do that. Then you have your own space." Mathew offered thinking it would be a good suggestion.

" Really? Are you sure you'd want to do that? It's not a big deal to just come out and go into the other room." Faith did like the idea of the adjoining door, but she didn't feel like it was really needed.

" I'm most certainly sure. This is your home too now, and it'd make it more convenient for you to have that doorway."

" Then I accept, but let's wait until after Christmas, so we don't have to worry about all of that. I'm just wanting to focus on celebrating Thanksgiving and Christmas with you! Then we'll worry about any remodeling. As I have an idea for something to help make life more convenient for you as well." Faith said with a serious look.

" Sounds like a wonderful plan; Giving the holidays the focus due them. I have to ask, what do you have in mind for me with the remodel?"

" Grandpa, you need a walk-in shower. Getting in and out of a bathtub can be dangerous as we get older. I know that you're very capable now, but it would make me worry less if you just had a walk-in shower instead."

" That's not a bad idea, and it would make it easier. I guess we should make a list of everything we want to have remodeled before we call my contractor. We might as well do it all at once. As I'm sure there could be a few more adjustments made, to make it better for the both of us." Mathew walked over to Faith, and gave her a hug. " Thank you for looking out for your old grandpa. Also, and more importantly, welcome home."

Faith hugged him back, and said, " You're welcome, and thank you for giving me a home again."

" How about we have a cup of tea, and make a Christmas list? I'm finding myself excited to get a Christmas tree with lights and the works this year." Mathew suggested.

" Yes! I am too!" Faith said with an excited smile.

Their afternoon faded away with excitement, laughter and love.

Dinner was again made together, with the cup of tea after cleanup and a game of cribbage shared as well. Then they just relaxed in the living room sharing stories. Even Faith shared some childhood memories, with love and joy, instead of pain and grief.

Mathew really enjoyed the stories Faith shared, but really focused in on the hot cocoa after school routine, where she'd share her day with her mother. Mathew figured hot cocoa could be shared here too. It didn't have to always be tea. He knew Lovey would understand and be glad he made sure to honor Faith's times with her mother, as well.

She truly was home. She made sure to Thank God again for her new grandfather, and home. She never realized how much she needed both, but now she knew. Her entire life changed including her perspective.

Faith felt like she slept truly wonderfully the first two nights there. This night somehow felt even better, and more deeply, more peacefully, and more refreshing. She wasn't dreading anything the next day; no more hating the thought of going to her apartment.

Chapter Six

The next morning Faith thought this is crazy! Yet not in the way, she'd think normally. What she found as crazy, was how completely right it all felt. Logic would suggest moving in with another person, of any age, after only knowing them less than a week, would be insane. Or at the very least have some very strong circumstances forcing such drastic measures.

Clearly, Faith didn't have any problems, or issues living on her own, and supporting herself. Mathew didn't seem to require her help either. Yet here she is fully committed to moving in here, and was basically already living here. She just knew she wasn't going to be staying at her apartment another night. It was truly mind boggling how absolutely right this all felt.

Faith had people she'd known for years, and she never remotely felt as comfortable with them as she does with Mathew. She just instinctively knew him, like she'd known him her entire life. Calling him grandfather felt as correct as it was calling her mother, mom. Logically, it made no sense, however there was no denying the feelings. She didn't have an adverse physical reactions like any other time she moved someplace. She was having no anxiety, no racing heart, no pit in her stomach feeling, no second guessing, no tension anywhere in her body. Everything in her entire being told her this was exactly as it should be, even trusting Mathew completely.

Faith remembered something her mom said before, about when God's hands are involved, we just know it's right. She said logic wouldn't have any place when God put you where you're meant to be, because every fiber of your being just would know it was right. You'd feel it through your mind, body, heart and soul. Never fight it, or try to apply "our" limited logic to it. Just be grateful and cherish the gifts God has blessed you with.

" Mom, I never understood that until now. Thank you for all the wisdom you shared with me. I still remember even though I let my anger and grief of losing you keep me from the good memories too. I'm sorry I haven't honored you and the lessons you shared with me, by living the best life, you tired to give me. I promise to do better. I will show the world who you raised me to be. I will let God's love and importance in my life shine more brightly. Mom, I will lead with love always, just like you taught me. I do miss you. My life will be better now. I feel like you would be grateful and happy I've found family. I know it's not the family you always wanted me to have, but I think grandpa is the family I need. After I loss you, I closed my heart, and with grandfather it's opened up again. Speaking of grandfather, I should get up and join him for breakfast. I love you mom. I hope I'm finally making you smile and happy with how I'm starting to truly live now. I will talk to you again soon mom. " Faith wiped the tears from her face without having any shame about having cried.

Then she got up and went to start their daily routine, with a brightness within her entire being, and a smile on her face. She has true joy in her heart now, and it felt amazing.

" You look happy granddaughter." Mathew was so relieved to see her joyful this morning. He wondered, last night, if the reality of her moving in with him would make her second guess her decision.

" You know what grandpa, I am happy. I even talked to my mom this morning. I haven't even tried to speak to her since she passed away and went home to heaven. It was too hard, but now my heart feels open again. That is because of you, grandfather. Thank you for giving me a family again, and helping with healing my heart."

" Oh my sweet girl, you've done just as much for me. I was a little worried after you sat with the full realization of moving in here, you'd second guess your decision. I have to say I am so relieved to see you happy this morning. I do have to ask though, any second thoughts?" Mathew was sure she didn't have any, but wanted to give her an opportunity to speak up if she did.

" Sorry grandpa." Faith looked at him with a completely serious face.

Mathew's face tried to maintain just as it was, but he was a bit afraid.

" You're stuck with me!" Faith walked over and kissed his cheek with a grin.

Mathew chuckled. " Young lady, you gave this old man a scare with that one. You owe me a hug for causing me a moments worry."

" Of course, grandpa. Sorry, I could not help myself."

" Please never try to stop yourself from giving this old man a laugh. It's good for the soul." Mathew's heart was also so full of joy and love.

" I promise grandpa." Faith gave him a hug, and a warm smile full of love and joy. " How about we get started on breakfast? I'm hungry."

" Yes. I'm rather hungry as well." Mathew felt like this was a true miracle. Everything with meeting Faith, and her moving in was such an unexpected blessing and gift. It had to be a miracle sent directly from God.

It was something how Faith, and Mathew had such a smooth flowing routine after only a few days. Anyone watching would have thought they had have been doing this for years. That's how natural and right everything was with Faith being there.

It felt more correct to Faith, than anything else had since before her mother's passing.

Mathew was having that same feeling of correctness to Faith being a part of his life, and his family.

After breakfast they sat down to enjoy their mugs of hot tea, and their game of cribbage. Faith learned quickly, and they both enjoyed a game with their tea.

Faith headed over to her soon to be old place, to work on packing up the rest of her things, and make final arrangements after tea.

Mathew offered to go with her, and help, but Faith said she could handle the rest. Mathew didn't argue as he planned to sneak out while she was gone to do a bit of Christmas shopping, and he had some other matters he wanted to attend to as well.

Faith was glad he didn't insist, as she too planned a little Christmas shopping before she went to finish the packing. She had a nice little store that she just knew would have the perfect gift for him, and it was right on the way to her apartment.

She wasn't the only one who had an idea of exactly what she was looking for as a gift. Mathew too knew exactly what he wanted to get Faith as well.

Faith was right, she found exactly what she had in mind for her grandfather. Once again she thought about how crazy all of this is. Yet there was absolutely zero denying that she knew this was all exactly as it's meant to be. She knew this gift would have a special meaning, but she didn't know what yet. She just woke up knowing what she was looking for, and when she saw it, she knew without a doubt it was exactly what she was supposed to get him. She was actually looking forward to finding out the significance of it on Christmas.

Her heart heard, and felt her mother's love and joy over Faith's newly formed family, and life changes. It was something she never thought she'd experience again: Feelings of love, and joy without soul wrenching grief, while thinking about her mother. She couldn't help but to just stop, and feel grateful for that, and to give God thanks.

When Faith realized, while finishing up the packing in her apartment, that she had no emotional attachments to any part of this place she shook her head. She now knew without a doubt, that she stopped living life when her mother passed away. She felt ashamed for that. Everyday God blessed her with life, and everyday she kept her heart closed off, and didn't appreciate, value, or honor the gift each day was, and all it could be.

Faith promised not only God, but also herself, that she'd never again dishonor such a gift, God gave her each day. She even promised her mom, to truly live life again too.

She decided right then to live life in such a way that honors God's gifts, and the love and lessons her mother had given her. Then an understanding came to her; that she never would have known without all the miraculous changes in her life. Her mother's body passed away, and her soul went back home to Heaven, yet her mother would never be completely gone, because her love and lessons live everyday within Faith. She allowed all the feelings of grief, and those of pride and love came with them. For the first time she was able to allow the grief without feeling overwhelmed by it.

While Faith was busy packing, Mathew too had found exactly what he was hoping to find for Faith's Christmas gift. He was actually surprised how easily he had found it. Mathew knew he was being guided by a much higher power. His heart filled with love and gratitude. During breakfast he was given an idea of what to get his newly found granddaughter, and when he saw it, just as it was with Faith, he knew it was exactly the one. He couldn't wait to get to give it to her on Christmas.

Having found Faith's gift so quickly, Mathew had plenty of time to handle the other business matter he hoped to get to today, before Faith got home. He got back home before she did, so he even called the contractor to schedule for him to come over and discuss remodeling after the first of the year.

Overall Mathew felt like he had accomplished everything he wanted to get done. Some of the business paperwork would have to wait to be prepared, before he could fully finish that part of his plans, but he was happy with how easily and quickly everything had come together. It let him know with complete certainty, that he was doing the right thing. Only God can bring everything together so easily and completely.

Faith got home just as Mathew was putting water on to heat for tea. She quickly carried in the several boxes she brought with her, then she sat down to join Mathew for a late afternoon tea.

" Perfect timing Faith. I'm glad you're home to share a cup of tea with me." Mathew eyes had such love, Faith couldn't help but to feel it.

" So am I grandpa. Just what I was hoping to have when I got home." Faith kissed his cheek before sitting down.

" Glad I was able to have my timing down. How did packing go? Do you have much more to do?"

" Packing was so quick and went so smoothly that I'm done already. The movers will be there tomorrow to load everything up and bring it here. Then I just need to go back to do a final cleaning and walk through with the landlord. It happened to work out that they have a new tenant looking to move right into the apartment, so they aren't going to make me wait until the two weeks notice time frame to finalize my move out. Timing for all of this has been perfect. It's like God's hand have been moving everything into place exactly at the correct time. I can't help but feel like His hands have wrapped all this love around me, as He worked everything out for me. All I had to do was open my heart to allow it. It's truly amazing grandpa, I never would have believed it was all possible, if I wasn't here living it, and seeing it all myself."

" Funny you said that, because I was thinking much the same thing today. God's hands have certainly been busy in all of this. Such a remarkably amazing gift, and I'd like to give back to the world to honor it. I'm hoping and actually counting on you to help with that." Mathew thought asking this much of her would be difficult, yet it wasn't feeling that way at all.

" I'd be honored to help grandpa. What do you have in mind?" Faith's trust in Mathew was complete. She knew that she could trust him one hundred percent. Beyond her mother, Faith never had that trust with another person before now.

" Well, I got to thinking about our talk about Thanksgiving, and making extra to share with those in need, and I'd like to expand that to all year. Maybe even find other ways to do more. We already came up with a name and a business plan even. I started getting it in motion today. It would be an honor to have your name on it all as well, so we can go ahead and start our giving back organization now. What do you think? Are you ready and able to start this now?" Mathew was certain she'd say she was.

" Oh my goodness, grandfather, I can't believe you got the ball rolling already! Yes! Let's do it. I'm all in on doing more for those in need!" Faith was excited to get going on it as well.

" I kind of figured you'd say that. The bank will have the paperwork ready as soon as I get him all the information on you. They thought I was a little insane setting all this up, since I didn't know your full name yet. I guess it does sound crazy to others, but it feels like the most sane decision I've made in a long while."

Faith laughed just picturing the faces of the bank staff. " I bet they were shocked to say the least. We can go tomorrow, and get them everything they need, but I am contributing as well, grandfather. I have money set aside from my mother, that I was waiting to use in the best way, and this feels exactly like the right way!"

" How could I argue with you honoring your mother in such a loving and giving way?"

" Can I share some pictures with you grandpa, of her? I haven't looked at them for many years, and I'd appreciate some company when I do." Faith felt like having grandfather with her would make it easier to allow the emotions to come and not fight them.

" I would love to share those memories, and pictures with you." Mathew knew how emotional this was going to be for her, and he would be there to help her through it, with all the love and support she needed.

They had finished their tea, and moved to the living room couch. Faith opened her first photo album, and smiled with tears in her eyes.

" Oh my goodness!" Mathew said with shock.

" What's wrong grandpa? Are you ok?" Faith looked over to see Mathew with tears in his eyes and a small smile on his face.

" Your mother's name was Julie, wasn't it?" Mathew asked, yet it didn't really feel like a question. It was like he knew it already.

" Yeah. Did you know her?" Faith was in shock of some sort now as well.

" My Lovey delivered you. We were on our way home, and came across an accident and we stopped to see if we could help. I stayed with your dad until he passed away, before any other help could arrive. Promising him we'd make sure his wife, and child weren't alone. That we'd do what we could to help her and you. You came into the world a few minutes later. I held you as my wife got your mom settled." Mathew had a tear roll down his cheek, with the miracle of all of this.

" Your wife's name was Joyce. My mother gave me my middle name in honor of your wife. My mom told me the story many times. She told me of an amazing couple who stopped to help her and my dad. How you sat and tried to comfort my dad, and held his hand until he breathed his last breath. How Joyce deliver me, and comforted my mom after I was born." Faith had to stop for a moment, as at this point they were both crying.

" Your mother named you after my wife?" Mathew never knew that, neither did Joyce.

" Yes. My parents had my name picked out, but my mom knew my father would understand if she gave honor to your wife by changing the middle name they had picked out. That's how I became Faith Joyce. My mom spoke often of how she wished she could have found your wife, to let her know what a blessing she was to my mom in her greatest hour of need."

" Lovey wondered about you and your mom over the years as well. Now this is all coming together; why it felt like I've known you all your life. God connected us at your birth, and our souls recognized each other. God knew we needed each other again, and He brought us back together."

" God is great!" Faith agreed. " That's why I immediately felt a connection to you, and so comfortable with you, and even felt at home instantly. It wasn't about the house, it was all about that connection we had at my birth." Tears flowing freely, yet a smile on her face.

It was an amazing shock to them both, yet it really made everything make more sense at the same time.

" Grandpa you should know that your wife Joyce, made such an uplifting and wonderful impact on my mom, even in that short time. My mom would quote something she told her that night whenever she needed a little extra strength. My mom asked your wife, that night, how she was going to raise me, and go on all alone now. Your wife told her, " No matter how you feel, or what was going on, you just have to put your lipstick on, and get out the door." She said my mom had me, which is still apart of her husband, so his love still lived within me. That's how she could and would raise me and go on with life. That my mom would not dishonor the love of my father by doing anything else. It was your wife that saw my mom through losing my dad and having me all at once."

" That sounds exactly like my dear Joyce." Mathew let his emotions flow in the form of tears and a smile. To know Joyce made such an impact in Julie's life, made his heart overflow with love. He smiled at the memories of Lovey refusing to leave the house without her lipstick on, and one in her purse for touch ups when needed.

" My mom never stopped looking for Joyce when we were out anywhere. She told me the story over and over, and also told me that with my dad's love and with Joyce's name, life and God had great things meant for me. After my mom passed, I stopped believing that, but after meeting you, again apparently, I started believing that again." Faith broke down in such powerful emotions of love, understanding and joy.

Mathew simply wrapped his arm around her, and said, " I know. I feel it too," as he allowed those very feelings to overflow throughout his being as well.

" God works in such marvelous ways! My Joyce would look at every woman, looking to see if she would find your mother again. She couldn't believe with everything we all went through together that night, that we never found out such a small, yet big detail, as of each others full names. For a short while after that night Lovey, was upset that she didn't have a way to find you, and your mother. She thought you both could use a little extra love and support, but one day she was given an understanding. She told me God had you two. That Julie needed to have this time to see and know she still had everything she needed, not to just raise you, but to thrive in life. Joyce kept you and your mother in her heart and prayers, until the day she passed away. Although she always kept an eye out just in case, God let us cross paths again."

" You know what I think grandpa? I think your Joyce and my parents are up there together smiling that we are here together now." Faith smiled with so much love and peace.

" I think you are right about that; my heart is somehow even more over joyed with that image."

" It seems we have a lot of catching up to do grandpa. It's a really good thing I live here now." Faith said with a grin.

" It certainly is." Mathew kissed her cheek. " Funny to learn how connected our stories are. Makes sense now. It all felt right, don't get me wrong, but logically it seemed crazy, if you think about it. Did it seem the same way to you Faith Joyce?"

" Yes, I thought that very thing grandpa. However, I could not deny that it felt exactly right, and where I am meant to be. God does work in wondrous ways!" Faith loved that he used both her first and middle name. She wasn't sure she would want to hear her name spoken any other way now. After hearing grandpa say it with such love and pride, Faith now realized the legacy and love attached to them. She had a greater desire to honor both more fully.

" Love connects us all. It's not always the same way we love another, but it is always a powerful, pure, and perfect way." Mathew said.

" That's beautiful."

" For such an old man, I see, I still have so much to learn. It wasn't until that very minute that I realized and saw the truth in the way love connects us." Mathew had a look of awe in his eyes.

" Oh grandpa, I think that's part of living; learning new things as we grow, and change, as the world changes. Could you imagine how pointless it would all seem if we could learn and know all of everything early in life, or even in our golden years?"

" Now that you say that, I can see that you're absolutely right."

" Life, love, learning are all a part of the journey. It's up to us how we apply our faith to them that makes it truly priceless, and beautiful. I think God brought us back together so I could see that."

" You're not the only one who needed to reconnect with you to see and learn some valuable lessons." Mathew replied open and honestly.

They looked at each other with a new understanding in the power of God's love.

" Thank God, for seeing the big picture and having divine timing and intervened perfectly." Faith said after a moment. "

Because I could not imagine life without having known you grandpa."

" My life is definitely all the brighter, and richer having you in it. Knowing you now, I couldn't imagine my life without you in it either, Faith Joyce."

They spent the rest of the day sharing more stories, which now had a deeper meaning and connection to them both.

There were tears shared, laughs had, and so much love felt.

Faith even openly shared about her mother's illness and death, and how angry she stayed about it, until reconnecting with him. She had to stop and get her emotions under control many times, but Mathew understood, and gave her all the time she needed. Faith was able to grieve in a healthier way now. Faith could feel how important it was to share all of it with Mathew, and have his love and support, to help her with the grief she never fully allowed before.

Although they both felt like they were happy in their lives, they now knew exactly what was truly missing. Happy isn't really happy without a love filled life that makes a joyful heart. They both knew God's love, but now they realized the true power His love gave. They both had in different ways moved away from God's love and all the joy that came with it. When God reconnected them, He also reconnected them to His love.

They planned on working to show others the power of having God's love in your heart and your life. The simple fact was if Faith didn't know and have God's love in her heart she would have never gone to check on Mathew at the hospital.

If Mathew didn't have and know God's love, he would have just sent Faith away at the hospital.

If they hadn't had known God and His love, and have those strong roots, they could have missed this remarkable gift God gave them. Life and loss took them a little off, the pathway God had made for them, but with those strong roots they were guided back onto the right path, and back to God's endless love, and a greater purpose.

It's God's love that made them care enough to get to talking after they collided in the store. God always opens doors for us, but if we don't know His love, we wouldn't know to walk through those doors. We could miss all the amazing and wondrous stops in our journey in life.

Chapter Seven

The next weeks seemed to fly by, with all the planning and work to get their giving endeavor all set up and ready to start on Thanksgiving Day. Between Mathew and Faith they had hundreds of ideas, so after they had everything all set for the first giving day, they went ahead and kept planning the next week, and for months after the New Year. By Thanksgiving Day they felt confident that they had all the bases covered, and could just enjoy their own meal without stressing or worrying about every detail, for the start of the love they hoped to share with others.

They enjoyed a lovely lunch, packed up the extras, and headed out to their first stop. With each meal they handed out, they also handed out a letter, and a small bag of necessities. Everyone was so grateful, and many couldn't stop tears of joy, and pure emotion from flowing. The letter was short and to the point:

God loves you. He sent us to show you He sees you.
Enclosed are a few gifts of love to help you in your
time of need. There's a number you can call if we
can help you find the next chapter in your life.
With love,
The ReJoyce in Faith Jules Gospel

They even made sure that they helped those who couldn't read the letter, without making it obvious. They tried to be loving and compassionate, so they didn't make anyone feel ashamed or anything other than cared about.

Mathew had come up with the name of their organization, and although they loved the first name they had come up with, they agreed this one seemed to fit and feel right. As it encompassed their family fully, and was a nod to those gone, who were just as much as part of this as they are.

The plan was all in place that anyone that called would be given as much help as they could, to help them get a fresh start. Of course, both Mathew and Faith knew some of those who called wouldn't be truly interested in helping themselves, but just had their hands out. They planned steps to weed out those people, so the funds would go to those who really wanted to start a new and better chapter. Sadly, not everyone wanted better. They thought those were the people who didn't accept God's love. Without love they simply wouldn't be able to help.

It was a long and emotional day. By the time they got back home, they were emotionally drained, but they also felt the overwhelming power of the love they got to bring to others. Overall the day gave them even more reasons to be grateful and happy to be able to give back, and share the love God's shown them.

" Are you all right Faith Joyce?" Mathew asked as they sat down to enjoy a hot cup of tea.

" I am. It was definitely a long day, and hard to see so many struggling as they are, but it felt good to bring a little love into their day."

" Yes, it was hard to see, but hopefully they'll reach out first to God, and then to us, and we can help with what we can. I think the hardest part was seeing the ones who thought God stopped loving them. I don't know why they think God abandoned them. The God I know would never abandon His child. We all make mistakes, and I realize some people make some really bad ones, but I think if they're truly good people and feel horrible about the things they did, they just need to turn to God to make things right." Mathew said.

" You're right grandfather. God never left them. It's us who denies Him. I know we don't always feel worthy of any love, let alone God's love, but everyone doesn't just deserve God's love, but we always have it. I'm going to pray tonight that all those who have denied themselves God's love, forgives themselves and open their hearts, minds, and souls back up to feel what has always been there for them; God's unconditional love."

" That my granddaughter is a beautiful and priceless prayer. I, too, will pray for that tonight. What a wonderful change would happen if everyone accepted and knew of the love God give us. Maybe our " giving endeavor " would not be needed, or not needed as much as it is. Could you picture a world full of everyone knowing, living, and sharing in the love God gives?" Mathew's heart almost felt like it was feeling a world just like that, and was reaching out for it. Mathew wondered if that was how God felt each moment of each day? As God know's what is possible within His love.

" I can almost feel it, but until that day comes we will work towards showing others that possibility. Maybe that way, the love and light that is God, will shine more brightly, and reach even further, until one day that love and light floods the world." Faith said not just as a wish, but also a promise to always keep working for that very thing. She felt it was the very least she could do, to honor all the gifts she'd been given and has.

God bringing her and grandfather together changed her life. In many ways it saved it. Denying every true feelings of

God's love within her heart, was like refusing to let it beat. God's love was what gave life meaning and purpose, without either of those she was not really living. She was going through the day to day requirements, but the best and most beautiful part of life was missing, so her life didn't feel like it had meaning or purpose.

They sat silently for a while just lost in their own thoughts.

" Well, grandfather, that, I'd have to say has been a perfect way to spend Thanksgiving. A truly lovely meal together, and then hours of giving in God's name. I'm drained and exhausted, but I'm excited to spend tomorrow, the next day, the next week, and even the next years doing it again, and again."

" I couldn't agree more!" Mathew said with a smile.

" It feels really good to share God's love, knowing we are witnessing for Him, and doing His work, by sharing and spreading His love. I feel like I've figured out my purpose here in life. I know that the world requires we work and do other things, but this feels like I'm serving a deeper, and more meaningful purpose now." Faith wasn't sure if she was expressing herself in a way that was making any sense, but she couldn't explain it any better.

" I've had that exact feeling more than once, so I know what you're saying." Mathew thought back to one particular time he felt that way. It was the day he and his wife helped Faith's parents, and delivered her into the world. Once again, Mathew got a glimpse of the big picture as it's come together, with them meeting again, and now doing this giving endeavor together. He knew he'd never stop being in total awe of God's amazingness, as it still managed to surprise him, even at his age, and he's known God and His love all his life.

" I think our purpose can change as we fulfill them." Mathew thought out loud.

" God made us, so there could be endless possibilities of what we are meant to do in our lifetime." Faith said in agreement.

" Very true. With God's love the possibilities are limitless."

" Do you think love will ever stop being able to lift us this high?" Faith asked almost rhetorically.

" Or to stop taking us by surprise? No Faith Joyce, I doubt it'll ever cease to surprise us and lift us to the greatest heights. It's a wonder, that I'm not sure we will ever fully grasp the full depths of its power." Mathew said with the same awe and wonder they were both feeling.

They had a relaxing and reflective rest of the night. Feelings of peace, and gratitude mixing with love was flowing strongly through them, and made them just want to sit quietly, to just allow the feelings to flow freely.

Chapter Eight

The next few weeks they had a lot of new ideas, and they found themselves busier than they thought they'd be. Yet they always made sure to have their quiet time to just relax with a cup of tea together, and one game of cribbage.

The ReJoyce in Faith Jules Gospel had not just been busy helping those that they could, it had also been able to make a huge impact. They'd also been able to gather others willing to help with the movement. There were even plans under way to open a short term housing unit to give those starting over the best chance.

Mathew and Faith were absolutely moved by the outpouring of support by so many others. This " little endeavor " of theirs was getting huge, and held the promise of making a really big impact for many more than they thought possible.

The love and gratitude they felt was priceless, and inexplicable. Each morning they'd pray for God's guidance as they'd make moves to be a source of love and light. Just as each night they'd say a prayer of thanks for getting to be that source of love and light, and being able to bring some of it to others.

One morning after continual influx of support Faith had to say her surprise out loud. " Grandpa, I know that I shouldn't be, but I'm so surprised by the amount of donations and support we're getting. The world has seemed so full of angry and hate filled people. I was honestly believing it had more evil in it than good. Now I see how wrong I was. It's like the evil was working through the media to make us all feel that way, so it could grow and spread more hate. Now however, I see that people are more good and wanting to share in spreading God's love, and light. Evil sure had me fooled, and made me feel almost hopeless."

" You weren't alone in that Faith Joyce. I guess someone just needs to give others a way to stand up and shine. Evil will always work to deceive. I think as long as we stand up with love and light, as an example, others will do so as well." Mathew replied.

" Evil made me think that putting any good into the world would just put myself under attack. I will never fall for that again. As I know God's love and will trust in Him always."

" All we can do is let our love and light that we get from God, shine brightly, and evil will never be able to reach our souls." Mathew was always a believer, yet this new chapter with Faith had taught him some very valuable lessons.

" Very true." Faith agreed fully with him.

After a nice breakfast and their cup of tea and game of cribbage, Faith headed to her office area to do her normal job. She was still able to get so much done, and was finding a new found joy in the work she was doing.

She had always known she was good at her job, but she never felt this joy within the tasks like she was now. In fact, everything she did now, she had that same new found joy. Nothing felt like a chore now, even the everyday job of doing dishes now felt like a blessing, and brought joy in doing them.

Connecting on this deeper level with the love and light of God, changed her entire perspective. Instead of being bothered by endless household chores, she found them as blessings, which gave her gratitude. She was seeing them as blessings, as she had dishes to do because she had food to eat. Laundry to do, because she has clothing to wear. It seemed like an obvious way to think of things in life, yet she had never realized it until she came into Mathew's life and truly reconnected to God.

Changing her perspective completely changed Faith's approach to each day and everything she did throughout them. Faith was also able to remember her mother, and the times they shared together now with love and joy. She no longer blocked the memories. Each memory that came to mind, were cherished and didn't make her feel like her heart was breaking all over again.

Faith said an extra thank you in her nightly prayers, that God intervened and brought Mathew back into her life. She wanted to believe that she would have come back around to feeling God's love at some point, but she would forever be grateful God gave her a helping hand. She already missed too much time and of living.

Even life's day-to- day had changed for Mathew. He had a new lease on this last chapter of his life. Before reconnecting with Faith, he thought he'd just have a quiet and uneventful rest of his life. Now together they started this foundation to give back and share love. It seemed to grow and develop more each day. It was keeping them both busy, and was becoming a big part of his day-to- day routine.

It touched Mathew's heart seeing so many others wanting to help and give back, to others in need as well. Like Faith he never considered the overwhelming generosity of others, would come flooding into the foundation. They never even thought that others would see them out giving, and that they'd find ways to donate or give. When they started this, they hoped to have enough to go for at least five years, but now it's gained enough support to go for double that. Not just that, but also gave them the ability to do more even.

Mathew thanked God each day for the new support and help. He was in awe with each new offer to help. Every day seemed to bring a new miracle, which Mathew knew could only be the work of God's hands and love. As that is from where all miracle came.

Due to all the extra donations they were blessed with, the foundation was going to be able to do so much more for others over Christmas. Both he and Faith had been spending every free moment they could preparing for all they were going to do. They hardly had time to even decorate their own house. As much as they enjoyed being able to help share God's love and light with others, they were both relieved to have finished with all the foundation work last night, until after Christmas at least.

They were both very much looking forward to some much needed time to just enjoy the Christmas season as well.

Chapter Nine

They were both excited to start with the Christmas decorating the next day. At breakfast they decided to see what all they both had for decorating. Then they'd make a list of the items they still wanted. They had already made the list for the meals for both Christmas Eve, and Christmas Day. They both agreed that celebrating the birth of Jesus deserved both days.

Neither Mathew nor Faith had much in the way of decorations. It made them both realize what all they stopped doing properly, when they loss, his wife, and her mother. They both vowed to do better from that moment until the day they joined back with their loved ones in heaven.

" It's going to be very busy grandpa, with the official Christmas shopping season upon us. It is up to you, but if you'd rather just send me with the list, I wouldn't blame you." Faith felt like she should offer, although she was fairly certain he'd want to come with her, and she'd rather he did too.

" Aww, you're very sweet and thoughtful, my amazing granddaughter. Thank you for offering, but I'd very much like to go with you. I know it'll be a mad house, but hopefully everyone is feeling the Christmas spirit, and is sharing it with kindness and consideration."

" I'll love the company, and I hope you're right about everyone sharing the Christmas spirit in the right ways."

The stores were all very busy, like they figured they'd be, but everyone was sharing that Christmas spirit in all the best ways. It was heartwarming getting to witness the kindness and consideration of all those around them. They had no problem finding all the things they wanted, a beautiful blue spruce fake tree and tree skirt to reuse over the years, five boxes of colorful lights, angel and star themed ornaments, and candles to place in the windows. They had an angel for the top of the tree already that was Joyce's favorite decoration, and Faith had kept her mom's favorite ornaments as well. They figured they had everything they needed and went to check out.

When they stopped for lunch after finishing all the shopping, both of them had smiles on their faces, and even more love within their hearts.

They thanked God for that heartwarming experience while saying grace.

" The media and people in power want us to focus on all the hate in the world. After seeing so much kindness from so many this last month, and even today, I can see the devils hands in those reports. There truly is so much good and love in the world." Faith expressed with a hopeful and peaceful heart.

" Wouldn't it be something if the technology failed, and people had to rely completely on what they heard, saw, and felt by themselves? The way it used to be. I think that would certainly slow down the spread of hate and evil, that the devil sends out through these media reports. I know I'm an old man, and I don't understand why people are into being on these social media things, but I can tell you that not all advances in technology have been good. Times were more simple in many ways, before internet. It breaks my heart sometimes of all the wonderful things the younger generations are missing. They never look anywhere but those darn phones, they miss all the everyday miracles right in front of them." Mathew knew

Faith would understand, even though she is one of the younger generations.

" Maybe we can help try to bring back some of those wonderful things within our foundation? Make it part of our mission: Bring back a more simple time, so that others can connect to what's really important, and what matters the most." Faith had never even considered something like that, but as the words came flowing to her, she knew the importance of making it happen.

" I love that, Faith Joyce." Mathew smiled.

" Me too, but I honestly cannot take credit for it. The inspiration just hit me. However, I cannot deny the importance of trying to do just that. Maybe in doing this, it'll help others see the love and light within the world more as well. It's also always a good thing to stop the devils work." Faith smiled back at him.

" Agreed! I will always stand to help share more love and light, but to also stop the spread of hate and evil. By sharing more love and light, we limit the power evil has to spread. That's always worth standing up for, and I will do it until my last breath."

" Me too grandpa. Me too." Faith knew, just as Mathew did that it's not always easy, but it matters.

They had a nice lunch, both thinking on how best to implement this new addition to their mission.

Mathew was wore out by the time they got home, so Faith told him to go take a nap. She promised to wait to start decorating until he was rested and ready.

While Mathew was napping Faith wrapped his gift to have it ready to go under the tree. Then she started writing down ideas that would honor this added mission, they've been blessed enough to be given.

She had no shortage of ideas that came to her: Coloring/drawing books with color pencils, journals for people write inside with pens, family board games to suit all age levels, good clean books for every age to help people reconnect with the goodness in the world, see things can be better, and to ignite the imaginations of all ages, and even a family recreation night once a month, or more if they could find a place and have a budget for it. If they had volunteers they might be able to add other things as well with learning crafts like knitting, painting, and all kinds of possibilities. Faith knew people had endless gifts that they'd need others to help nourish and develop as she wasn't one of those crafty type of people. Yet she always admired those who were. She thought maybe they could even do like craft shows if they get enough people making things, to help give them a little more income and pride in themselves.

It would definitely take a lot more work, and more time. Yet they both felt is was another gift they've been given. How could doing work for God be consider in any other way?

They both understood the responsibility that laid in their hands, and took it very seriously, yet approached it with gratitude, and humility. It wasn't about them, and they knew it. It's about God, and His love only. By knowing that, and keeping that as the focus, they knew they would succeed.

Both believed it was when people stopped remembering those things, that's when the devil would make it a tool for the use of corruption and hate. The gifts and talents we've been given are always meant to be used for sharing and spreading God's love. When you think it's all about your own glory, and success it gets corrupted, and becomes the opposite of the purpose of why God gave you those gifts.

By the time Mathew got up from his nap, Faith had been given so many ideas and inspiration on how to incorporate this new mission into the foundation, and had the plans all written up for Mathew to go over. She had them on the table where they'd sit for their afternoon tea, before starting on the decorating.

" My goodness!" Mathew exclaimed when he saw all Faith had come up with while he napped. " You've been busy. I didn't think I'd sleep that long." He joked, with a smile.

" Oh, I was rather surprised by it all coming to me that quickly as well. I guess that's how you know you're on the right pathway. As God gives us all we need exactly when we need it." Faith said with such heartwarming emotions.

It wasn't just one emotion Mathew could feel in those words. It was love, courage, strength, gratitude, joy, and peace all at once. Just hearing and seeing it from within Faith's voice and eyes, made it so Mathew could feel it all too.

It made him think of his dear wife, Joyce, as he remembered seeing and hearing all of that from her as she spoke with others of God's love. He silently thanked God again, not just for having sent him Faith, but also for these cherished memories having her in his life, brought back into focus. He was grateful for the memories.

Mathew always felt like he knew God and His endless love, but now he realized that God's love is something we, as humans, will never fully grasp the full depths.

Faith was feeling that same understanding of never being able to understand the all encompassing depths of God's love.

It was a very humbling understanding that came with an unmeasurable amount of gratitude.

They decided to go over the new ideas for the added mission of the foundation after they decorated. It had been too many years of not going full out with decorating and they were excited to get everything out, and the lights shining bright. It would be good for them to both put the light, love, and joy back into the reason for Christmas. Another thing they vowed to never stop again. They would always take time to honor and celebrate Christmas the way it always should be.

Oh my goodness, the love and laughter that filled the house as they decorated was music not just to God's ears, but also Joyce and Julie's.

They both shared stories. Mathew told the story of when Joyce came across the angel tree topper, and they argued as Joyce said money had better places to go, but Mathew saw how much it moved her, and refused to leave without purchasing it. He chuckled about how silly they must have seemed arguing in front of this beautiful angel tree topper. He said after all they argued about it, Joyce thanked him with tears in her eyes for not listening, as she truly did want it, and would cherish it each year.

Faith shared how she loved the stories of each ornament, that her dad had gotten for her mom, were told each Christmas before being placed on the tree. Julie shared those stories each Christmas to try to help Faith get a feeling of what a thoughtful, loving, and giving man her dad was. Faith shared each story exactly like her mom did before hanging each precious ornament on the tree. It wasn't really the ornament that was so precious to her mom, Faith realized now while sharing the stories with Mathew; it was the cherished memories, that's what was really being placed on the tree in honor of the love they shared.

After the tree was all set, and every decoration had been placed, both Mathew and Faith placed the gift they had for each other under the tree. When they both saw each other doing the same thing they laughed even more.

" Great minds think alike, so they say." Faith said through the laughter.

" I guess sweetheart." Mathew was laughing as well.

Then they just sat down to enjoy all the new lights and love spread around the house. It felt like they had Joyce, Julie and even Faith's dad with them, now that they shared the stories and had the special ornaments and topper placed.

" Grandpa, I have an idea. It's kind of odd."

" What's that Faith Joyce?"

" I think we should place one more gift under the tree each year for Jesus and God. It will be what goals we met with the foundation in Their names, and the next goals we will be working towards for the next year. I know God knows all we do and have done, but I think it will be a wonderful way to show our praise and gratitude for the honor of allowing us to serve in this very special way." Faith had tears in her eyes, but they weren't from sorrow. They were of love and joy.

Mathew did as well. " I think that's not just a beautiful idea, but also a perfect way to say thank you each Christmas. An amazing way to honor such a loving and amazing gift we've been given."

" I will be right back grandpa." Faith suddenly knew just how to do it as well.

She came back holding a beautiful leather bound scrap book. Mathew didn't ask, he waited for Faith to tell him. He could see the emotions held within her eyes. He knew this book held a sentimental connection.

" This was the last gift my mother gave me. She had hoped I'd fill it with my lifetime of cherished moments. As you know I did very well at blocking them before now, so I never felt like I had any thing that would honor her memory worthy enough to place in here. Now, I think this is the perfect way to use it. Each year we'll add to it, and place it under the tree." Faith had a few tears slide down her cheeks.

Mathew had her sit down next to him, and held her hand in comfort. He understood how emotional this was for her.

" I think your mother would be very pleased by that. I have a feeling she's already smiling down at you, feeling honored by such a beautiful gesture." Mathew assured her.

" I think so too, grandpa." Faith paused to gather her thoughts. " You know, grandpa, I used to think the bumps in the road were there to make me work harder, or that I somehow failed. Now I see that not all bumps in the road are meant for anything like that. They're there to help get us back onto the correct pathway. It's God's way of guiding us to the pathway meant for us, when we lose our way. Sometimes, I don't think we even realize that we've lost our way, until God guides us back to the right path."

" I never considered it that way, but hearing you say it like that, I think you're right." Mathew gave her hand a gentle squeeze.

" When I first ran into you with my cart at the store, I felt like I failed, but now I see God just made sure to get me back on the right path, because I was very lost. I didn't know it then, but I can see just how lost I was now." Faith admitted unashamedly. She refused to feel bad about the past, and to just move forward with love, joy, and gratitude.

" I can say the same. Looking back I was given bumps in the road, but like you I didn't see it as a guiding hand, and fought to stay on the same bumpy road. I have been lost too in a way, and I can see why God had to intervene to bring you into my life. It was the only way to get me back onto the correct path as well." Mathew wasn't ashamed to say that he had gotten a little lost as well.

" I thank God everyday for His *Divine Intervention* that gave me you." Faith gave Mathew a gentle kiss on his cheek.

Mathew nodded and smiled. " Me too, Faith Joyce, everyday."

It wasn't too long that they just quietly enjoyed the lights and love filing the room before they had to get at dinner.

Those feelings of light and love stayed within both of them the rest of the evening.

Chapter Ten

The time leading up to Christmas was wonderful for Mathew and Faith, although it was busy with all the new ideas for the foundation. They had figured out a few things to implement right away. They were also still gaining more help and funding from so many different sources.

They had put out some information to get some additional funding so the foundation could continue for many years, but the overwhelming amount of support was nothing short of a miracle.

They had developed a wonderful routine of working on foundation things at a set time, her work would be at another set time, and then they evenings would be just time for them to reflect on the love and light each day gave them.

Christmas Eve was here before they knew it. That day and Christmas Day was meant to celebrate God and the birth of Jesus. No foundation work, or anything else work related. It was a deal they made. As amazing as the gift of the foundation is, they didn't want it to make them forget to take time to celebrate and honor from where it all came.

These two days are meant to stop and honor the birth of Jesus, and the love of God, with family and friends. Since it was just the two of them, they decided to invite some others for Christmas Eve, that they knew would be alone. The list included waitresses, cashiers that they'd both gotten to know over the years, and long time friends of Mathew and Joyce's.They had a house full for dinner. The love and joy was a shared blessing to all of them. Especially to those who thought they'd be alone for all of Christmas. Some of them in attendance even made plans to spend Christmas Day together as well, so they wouldn't be spending Christmas Day alone now.

Christmas morning was just for them, but Christmas Evening they again invited others who would be alone. They agreed that they had so much to give, it should be shared, and they both knew what spending Christmas alone felt like. Being able to give others someone to be with was the least they could do. The Christmas Day meal list included some more long time friends of Mathew and Joyce's, the contractor they were going to hire after the first of the year, a few of those who had reached out to try to give to the foundation, and even one of the nurses from Mathew's hospital stay. All people who would have otherwise spent the day alone.

They had a very nice and relaxing breakfast, and made sure to take time for their morning cup of tea, and game of cribbage. However this morning Mathew surprised Faith with a cup of hot cocoa instead. He felt it was important to bring back a little of that tradition for Faith this day.

Faith was moved to tears by his loving and thoughtful gesture, yet she was so grateful to honor that tradition her mom had with her this morning. Now it really felt like Christmas complete with her mom too.

After they cleaned up they went into the living room to exchange their gift.

" Grandpa would you mind if we start with the gift for Jesus and God first?" Faith asked when they reached the living room.

" I was thinking the same thing. It seems like the most important gift, and should be given first." He smiled at her, glad they were thinking the same way.

Faith grabbed the beautiful book, and sat down by Mathew to look at it and honor the greatest gift they've been given as well.

" Dear Father, and our brother Jesus, this gift is meant to thank You, and honor the blessings You have given us in working and giving in Your name. It is small, in comparison to all You have given us, but the thought, and love behind it is great. Merry Christmas. With all our love, honor and praise." Faith spoke the words out loud and then looked to Mathew to see if he wanted to add anything more.

" Amen." Was all he added.

Then they took time to look at the two pages they added. One of what they did, and the other was of next years goals for giving.

They laughed at some of the memories, as they went through each one, and cried at other memories. Then prayed for guidance for each goal, for the next year.

It felt like the perfect way to honor this gift, and to be thankful for all they'd been given. They had some time with just a few moments of silence as well.

" Ok, time for me to give you your gift, from me grandpa." Faith went to get his gift from under the tree.

" Will you please grab yours as well, Faith Joyce?" He asked.

They agreed to one gift each, as they felt they'd been given so much already.

Each of them wanted the other to go first, but Mathew gave into Faith, to open his first. He realized that he couldn't deny her anything.

Mathew was speechless, and tears ran freely down his face, when he saw the pocket watch Faith had gotten him.

" Oh no, grandpa." Faith was worried she hurt his feelings somehow, but when he looked up into her eyes, she knew that wasn't the case.

" I don't know how you were led to get me this, but it's beyond perfect." He took a moment to gather himself, before sharing the story behind his strong emotional reaction. " My Lovey gave me a pocket watch exactly like this, the first Christmas after we were married. She had spent many hours secretly doing mending to get the money for it, as she felt like it would mean more that way. I couldn't believe she'd done that for me, and I was moved to my very core. I loved and cherished that watch for years. I never left the house without it. It was the night you were born that we got home, and I couldn't find it. I tried for days to go everywhere I had been the day I had lost it, to see if I could find it. I was heartbroken, but my Joyce said it was okay. She said God must have found someone in greater need of it, and made sure to get it into those hands."

Faith found it all made sense suddenly. " I was given this idea to look for a gift for you at this one certain place, an antique shop, and once I saw it, something, or someone said, 'that's it.' I never questioned it, but now it all makes complete sense. I think Joyce wanted you to have it back to remember that God's timing is never wrong."

" Sounds just like her." Mathew smiled, and knew Faith was right. Joyce definitely had a hand in this, as did God. He would never doubt the power behind God's love, or those already in heaven, watching over them. " Now it's your turn, Faith Joyce. Go ahead and open your gift." Mathew was wondering if Julie and God had a hand in her gift as well.

" I have to be honest, I'm a little nervous, seeing what God and our loved ones have been up to this year." Faith said with both wonder, and such love. " I feel like I've already been given so much grandpa, I think this would seem like too much, no matter what it is."

" I know what you mean, I felt the same way, but I think you'll see that there's a reason for it once you open it." He said, as he just knew now that there would be a special meaning behind the gift he was led to get her.

Once Faith opened her gift, Mathew knew he was correct. There was a personal story attached to his gift for her as well.

Faith started crying and laughing at the same time. Mathew just gave her the time to gather herself, just as she had done for him, before she could tell him the story behind the gift.

Mathew's gift to her was an antique nurses watch, that you pin onto a shirt or sweater. He too was led to a certain store, yet different antique shop than the one Faith went to, to look for her gift. When he saw it he was told, just as Faith was, "That's it". Now he was patiently waiting to hear the significance behind this particular watch.

" Grandpa, all I can say it's a very good thing Joyce and my mom are in heaven working for God, instead of against, because these two could cause some mighty big trouble together."

Mathew laughed, he couldn't argue with her logic. " You're probably right, on that."

" This watch, or one exactly like it, belonged to my mom's mom, my grandmother. My mom would get it out from time to time when she was missing her mother. I never got to meet me grandma. I'd watch my mother when she'd get it out. When she was looking at it, it would somehow make her feel better. Like she was given an answer to whatever was weighing on her. When times got really hard, my mom told me she had to sell grandma's watch. I felt really bad for her, as I knew it meant so much to her, and I said that to her. My mom told me that she knew it would find it's way back to me at the exact time it was meant to. She explained the watch still meant a lot to her, but the memories would still be with her, even if the watch wasn't. I asked her how she could believe that it would end up finding it's way back to me. She looked at me with such love, and honesty, and said that was simple: Faith. Having me gave her faith everyday to have the strength to do what she must. My father picked my name because it was faith that brought them together as they met at a church social. I never felt like my name held so much meaning for them, but after her death I had forgotten about the story behind her trust in this, and why my dad gave me the name I have. Seeing this watch brought back so many memories, that I had forgotten. She was right. It did find it's way back to me at the exact right time, and I truly understand the meaning my name held for them."

" God is great." Was all Mathew could think to say, yet it said it all.

The gifts, they were led to get for each other, held great personal meaning from their past. That now connected their present time together. More than all that they symbolized the love God gave them, when He intervened to bring them together.

They both spent time silently with their loved ones, and in prayer for the miracles God had given them with, not just bringing them together, but also showing them that there is so much more ahead of them.

This crazy journey finding their way back into each other's lives, and even finding those perfect gifts all fit together now. Sometimes in life we can just feel things, without understanding of why, yet have no doubt in them. Each step in their journey from the moment Faith hit Mathew with her shopping cart, to the Christmas gifts all happened because they both could just feel it was right. No logic played a roll in it, but for them it was as true, right and pure as love it self, because God's love was the guidance in each step. It was rather mind-blowing to them both now that they saw the full picture, and they were grateful and in wonder of the miracles God gave them.

They knew they would have the time to do all the work they planned together, in God's name. It all made perfect sense now, to them both! They would never question *Divine Intervention,* again, as God's timing is always perfect!

Epilogue

The next year at Christmas, there were still only three gifts under the tree.

They still had the album with what they accomplished, with the foundation, and added what they planned to accomplish with the next year. They had been blessed with a steady influx of support, with monetary donations, physical items, and volunteers. The foundation was growing more each month it seemed, and had become bigger than either of them ever dreamed it would.

They had even been able to purchase a building with office space, computers, and added volunteer teachers to help those who needed more education. The building even had a floor, of small, but safe apartments that were used as step housing for those willing to put in the work and get off the street. They'd already had many move in, maintain work enough to move out into their own rentals, which gave them an extra sense of pride.

Faith still did her normal day job to keep her income, and never mixed the two, even though when she had extra, she would donate it into the foundation, secretly. Mathew had found a new purpose with running the day to day in the office, and maintaining the foundations schedules, and adding more volunteers and programs as they could.

Even as busy as life had become, they still came together each morning and evening to share meals, and their normal cup of tea and/or hot cocoa, and game of cribbage. It was how they both decided worked best. Sitting together each morning before starting their days, and sharing their days together each night, gave them all they needed each morning and night.

They also still did the one gift each for one another. They had so much, and still felt like they had been given such an amazing gift already. Faith gave Mathew his gift first again. She had made him a special album with them, and some favorite phrases they shared, since meeting that had meant so much to her. She wanted him to know she would forever cherish each memory they've made together. She had even added a few angels throughout the pages to represent her parents, and Joyce. One page she made just full of photos of Joyce, and her parents, as they are as much apart of their story as Mathew and Faith are.

Mathew was moved to tears. The gift was perfect, and filled his heart to overflowing. Then he gave her the gift he'd made for her.

Faith wasn't sure what it was she was looking at first, as when she opened the box it was typed papers all clipped together. Then she read the first page, which didn't have much on it. It read:

<u>*Divine Intervention*</u>
<u>*God Puts Us*</u>
<u>*Where We're Meant to Be.*</u>
By: Mathew Gospel

" Oh my goodness! Grandpa you wrote a book!" Faith was smiling, and couldn't wait to read it.

" Read the next page Faith Joyce." Mathew said, giving nothing away.

Faith did as he asked. She read it out loud:

Dedicated to my amazing granddaughter brought back into my life, by God's divine timing. All glory to God above, as well as all my gratitude for giving us this time together. I love you Faith Joyce. You've been a blessing and a gift. The world is all the better having your light and love in it.
With all my love,
Your adoring grandpa

Faith couldn't speak. She was crying, so moved with love and joy. Once she was able to say anything, she couldn't find the words to express the depth she was feeling.

" This doesn't seem to be expression enough, but I don't know if there are words for it, but I love you grandpa. I'm honored and humbled. Also so very grateful for you as well!"

The rest of the morning they spent drinking hot cocoa, while Faith had Mathew read his words to her, as she wanted to hear the story in his voice to have yet another cherished memory.

Don't miss out!

Visit the website below and you can sign up to receive emails whenever Liv N. Love publishes a new book. There's no charge and no obligation.

https://books2read.com/r/B-A-LFSJD-FPDZF

BOOKS 2 READ

Connecting independent readers to independent writers.

www.ingramcontent.com/pod-product-compliance
Lightning Source LLC
Chambersburg PA
CBHW050751270225
22593CB00001B/60